Jenı So much
so she d. .ntil her
pillow mo

She t... very still and lifted her lids. A chin with a
rather strong looking jaw covered in a day old fair-haired
beard was barely a breath away from her face. This close
she had no trouble seeing the slight cleft faintly hidden
beneath the stubble.

With a gulp she lifted her head, dying to get a really
good look at Ian Southernland. Without her glasses she
had to be nearly nose-to-nose with the man to see him,
and this was her only chance, because she didn't believe
for one minute that they would find a peddler with
glasses, least of all one with any strong enough to make
much of a difference. Regardless of how many wishes she
made.

Praying Ian was still sound asleep, his deep
breathing hinting that he was, she let her gaze travel
along his powerful jaw across his features. She was
stunned, awed, and thoroughly amazed at how right Tuck
had been. He was the very image of her Prince Charming.
He was beautiful.

There was a hitch in his breathing and she suddenly
found a pair of startling blue eyes peering back at her.
She licked her lips as she struggled for something
coherent to say while her limbs had locked in place, but
what? Sorry I slept on you?

Those amazing eyes darkened, sending her good
sense to the farthest edge of the planet, and she pressed
her mouth to his. He was not appalled by her actions,
quite the opposite. Like a whisper, he teased and
tormented her with his lips, warm and soft, and full of
sin.

Rogue's Challenge

by

Jo Barrett

Rogue's Challenge

Contact Information: info@thewildrosepress.com

Cover Art by *R.J.Morris*

The Wild Rose Press
PO Box 708
Adams Basin, NY 14410-0706
Visit us at www.thewildrosepress.com

Publishing History
First Faery Rose Edition, 2008
Print ISBN 1-60154-257-7

Published in the United States of America

Dedication

This one is for all those wonderful readers who begged for the sequel. Thank you!

Prologue
Scotland, Isle Of Mull, Summer 1585

"I have lost my bloody mind," Ian Southernland grumbled.

"Second thoughts?" Colin MacLean asked.

"Nay, but 'tis a bit overwhelming," he admitted to his long time friend.

"Aye. But I wouldna' ask if Amelia wasna' certain that Jenny would be of help tae her."

Amelia MacLean, formerly Amelia Tucker, was Colin's wife and a dear friend of Ian's. She was in the last stages of her pregnancy and wished for her friend to be by her side at the birthing. Jenny Maxwell, however, was not only a female physician, but happened to reside in the twenty-first century, and it was Ian's job to fetch the woman back through time.

He rubbed his temple as they neared the spring.

"Are you not well, mon?"

"Nay, 'tis but a pain in my head from the bludgeoning of information Amelia has bestowed on me these past days. I only hope that I do not appear as...how did she phrase it?"

"Nutball. Aye, 'tis what she said."

Ian chuckled. "Not a flattering image."

They dismounted.

"I still cannot believe I am about to step into a bit of water and be transported through time. If I had not seen Amelia disappear myself one year past, I would never believe such a thing," he said as they neared the enchanted spring.

"Aye, 'tis a baffling thing. One has tae see it tae believe." Colin's face turned grim. "But I will understand if you doona wish tae do this thing, Ian. 'Tis no simple task we ask of you."

"Nay, I shall not waiver in my decision. But if I

1

should not return..." he let out a long steady breath.

"You will return." Colin slapped him on the back. "Aunt Elspeth has seen it. And her gift of sight has ne'er been wrong."

"Aye." Ian's shoulders drooped. "But 'tis what she has not seen that concerns me."

"All will be well, my friend."

Ian snapped his head up and straightened his spine. "Aye, and I shall return. And with Mistress Maxwell. I vow it."

"And I will be here."

With a nod Ian stepped toward the water.

"And doona take all day, you Sassenach," Colin called after him, his brogue thick with jest. "I've better things tae do than stand around this bleedin' spring waitin' for you."

An unsteady laugh escaped Ian's grim lips as he stepped into the burbling stream and everything around him, the very world he knew, vanished.

Chapter One
Scotland, Isle of Mull, Winter - Present Day

"Fascinating. If I weren't a scientist, I wouldn't have believed my very own eyes," Jenny murmured, adjusting her glasses. But it was true. Amelia Tucker, Jenny's bodyguard, her friend, was gone. She'd vanished the moment she stepped into the fountain. Jenny could only hope her time travel theory was correct and that Tuck would be sent back to sixteenth century Scotland to the man she loved, where she longed to be.

A shard of jealousy sliced through her as the cold night air snuck beneath her coat. Tuck had someone who wanted and loved her, while Jenny...

"It's of no consequence," she said on a long exhale. It was Tuck's chance at happiness, one she deserved. But would she ever have that same chance? Jenny shoved her hands deep into her pockets and started toward the car.

"Again, it's of no consequence. I have my work, my father needs—" she staggered over the words, tired of lying to herself. Her father didn't need her or want her. She was a commodity when her research proved fruitful for his company, but other than that, he didn't know she existed. His health was poor, but he still managed to run his empire from a wheelchair without any help from her.

Jenny paused and looked up at the star speckled sky. "I should've gone with Tuck," she whispered. She wasn't needed in the twenty-first century, not by her father, not by anyone.

There was no doubt she'd miss the ease of life in the present, the conveniences, and she did think that sixteenth century Scotland was a bit rougher than she'd like, but at least she would be with her friend. Someone who cared.

"Nonsense. As if Tuck needs a tag-a-long on her adventure. She has a man that loves her, a new family of a sort."

Jenny resumed her walk to the car, forgetting she was supposed to be stealthy as she crossed the vast gardens of Raghnall Castle. A fact brought rapidly to the forefront of her mind at the sound of a man shouting at her.

The night-guard! How could I be so stupid?

She bolted down the path, dodging left and right. She was horrible at lying and would babble nonsense like a fool if they caught her again.

On the fall equinox, when she and Tuck had stolen onto the property to test her theory about the fountain only working on the solstice, the guards had caught them. But thanks to Tuck's ingenious talent for quick responses when placed on the spot, the guards let them go.

The likelihood, however, of such an occurrence happening again and without Tuck in attendance was dismal at best. She'd have better luck regenerating dead tissue, she thought with a snort, then slid into a thick hedgerow, praying they wouldn't find her.

****

"This cannot be right," Ian murmured in the dark, deep within the shadow of a tall tree. According to Amelia, he was to appear in the daylight on an equinox, which equinox she was not certain, but 'twas most definitely supposed to be daylight. The location appeared to be correct, however, or so it seemed from her description. The tall statues and sculptured garden of Raghnall Castle surrounded him. Still, something was not as it should be.

He heard footsteps and decided his best option was to remain undetected until he could determine where and more importantly *when* he was.

"She went tha' way," a voice said nearby. "We'll corner her at the folly, there isna a way out from there." Gravel crunched beneath boots and separated, surrounding him. Ian had no doubt he was well concealed, but was curious as to who these men were.

The footsteps passed and he eased out of his hiding place. Could they be the guards Amelia had spoken of? If so, he needed to keep clear of them. But why would they be chasing a woman through the gardens in the dead of night?

A twig snapped and he froze. Breathing, faint but rapid, reached his ears. A smile teased his lips. Whoever she was she had evaded the sentries and doubled back. This female was leading them on a merry chase.

"She's no' aboot. Are ye sure ye saw her come this way?" one guard called to the other.

They were coming back. Ian moved silently toward the woman using her rapid breaths as a beacon. She was certain to be caught if she did not steady herself.

He paused a few paces away wondering what possessed him to aid this female. He knew nothing of her, of her reason for being here lurking in the dark on private property. Perhaps she was a thief of some kind.

Still, he had always felt the need to aid any woman in distress, and this one was most definitely in a bit of a spot. Outnumbered and alone, he could no more ignore his sense of chivalry as he could ignore the rising sun.

Egads! The sun! The telltale signs of dawn were visible on the horizon. They'd both be caught for certain if they did not get themselves away but soon. Quickly and silently he stole up behind her and threw one arm around her, pressing her back into his chest, while clamping his hand over her mouth.

"Shh. I mean you no harm, mistress." She struggled with surprising force considering her tiny size, and for a moment he thought her a child, for he had little trouble controlling her. "Be still. They are almost upon us."

The woman calmed, but only on the outside. Under his arm Ian could feel her racing heart beneath soft supple breasts. A grin tweaked the corner of his lips. Definitely no child. A shapely woman, albeit small, and one with a unique scent that teased his nostrils. He shifted, his cheek brushing the side of her head and sampled the silkiness of her hair.

"Where the devil can she have gone?" a guard asked grumpily, yanking Ian from his survey of the woman's form. What a dolt he'd become. Lusting after a woman he could not even see!

He had stayed too long without a bit of female companionship, but there was none at Arreyder he wished to acquaint himself with. He lived there, for the most part, and did not think it would be a comfortable situation should the lady or he have a change of heart at a later time. And with Colin happily homebound with his love, excursions about and abroad had ended. Thus, so were Ian's opportunities to seek his physical pleasures.

"Damned if I know where she could've disappeared tae," the other guard replied. "Didn't look like much of a cat burglar, though, from what I seen."

"Aye, ye may be right. Hey, think it was one of them women we caught some months back?"

One of the guards laughed. "Them loonies! Aye, I suppose it could've been. Or maybe one of the teenagers from the village again. Ye know how they get bored and dare one another tae do stupid things."

"Aye. Like the two of us once, eh?" They both chuckled as they walked past, their voices fading as they reminisced about times gone by.

Women some months past? Could I have arrived on the very night Amelia left the twenty-first century for the last time?

No, that could not be. He should have arrived on an equinox. And yet, he was supposed to arrive midday. This bore further consideration.

According to Amelia's friend, Jenny, a scientist as well as a physician, he should have stepped into the portal on the solstice in his time and out on the equinox in the twenty-first century. Then he merely needed to step into the fountain at Raghnall Castle on the next solstice to return to his own time arriving only moments after he'd left. Completing the trip, as it were.

And yet here he stood, in a time not his own, but in the cold of winter and at night. Interesting, to say the least, and a bit unnerving. Could it be that the portal was not linked to the person traveling, but to a schedule of its own? That in some way, he had completed Amelia's trip by stepping out on the solstice moments after she'd stepped in?

A distinct tapping at his arm, poking actually, drew his attention to the petite woman pressed against his chest. It could not be this simple, could it? Could his quest be completed with so little trouble? Is this slight female the very one he sought?

She poked him again with more vigor.

"I will remove my hand, mistress, if you promise not to scream. 'Twould be most unpleasant and would draw the attention of the sentries," he whispered. "Something I suspect neither of us wishes."

She nodded but hesitantly.

"On your honor?" he asked.

She huffed, bringing a faint grin to his lips. He slowly lifted his hand, ever ready to return it to her mouth if need be. But he had no chance to do so. With a movement far swifter than he would have suspected her capable, she elbowed him between the ribs and stomped with acute accuracy upon his large toe.

Ian lost his grip on her as he struggled for air. "I detect—the distinct—teachings—of one Amelia Tucker—in your proficiency, Mistress Maxwell," he wheezed.

Her steps faltered as she scurried out of his reach.

Aye, there was no doubt he had found the one he was seeking. Her hesitancy to flee at the sound of her name and her raw, although effective skills were proof enough. He had seen Amelia use and teach just such a technique to the ladies of his time so they might protect themselves to some degree.

"Did you follow us here? Of course you did. It's the only logical explanation," she said. "Well, whatever you saw, or think you saw, was merely a trick of the light. Nothing more."

"I am afraid you are mistaken," he said, straightening.

She took several slow steps backward. Not a good sign.

"I mean you no harm. On my honor." But his words were lost in the subtle breeze left from her dashing out of sight.

With a resigned sigh, and one very sore toe, Ian took after her. This was the best and possibly the only chance he would have to take the lady back to Amelia and Colin. He did not relish the idea of searching the globe for one lone female in a world not his own for six long months instead of the three he'd been told he would have. With luck the fountain would take them back in time this very eve.

If he could catch the little she-devil.

Dodging bushes, statues, and the occasional birdbath, he caught up with her. Unfortunately, not before she ran straight into the arms of one of the sentries.

"Oh! My glasses!"

"Quit yer squirmin'! Ye'll no' get away again," the guard said, and turned toward the castle.

"But my glasses," she said, continuing her struggle with the man.

A beam of light shot from the guard's hand and scanned the ground before them. Ian sucked in a breath and slid deeper into the shadows. Amelia had explained many things before he left, but to actually see the torch she'd described was truly amazing.

He turned his mind away from the tempting miracles he could experience in this time and debated his limited options on how to rescue the lady. Although he was a man who loved adventure and the opportunity to remain was becoming more and more intriguing, he would be most selfish not to complete his quest in as short a time as possible. Amelia needed this woman, and he vowed to bring her back in time.

"I doona see any glasses," the guard said, then flashed the light in the woman's face.

Ian had his first glimpse of the lady and frowned. This woman was a scientist? A physician? Amid the harsh light against the side of her face she appeared no more than a child. Perhaps he had the wrong female after all.

"Here, looks like Errol was right. Ye be one of them lassies from a few months back. Come tae take another midnight stroll, miss?"

Ian shook his head. That answered that question. Well, who was he to decide these things in this time? If a woman-child could be a physician, it was none of his business. All that mattered to him was Amelia's need of the lady. He would not break his vow to his friends.

****

Jenny blinked in the bright light. She'd known this would happen. Every coherent word had slipped away from her in the glare of the flashlight.

Think, Jenny! You have to get out of this. You're

8

father will be livid if word of this gets into the press, not to mention your reputation as a scientist! "I—I—uh—"

"Aye, ye can tell it tae the constable," the portly man said and turned.

"Dearest, I do hope you have not had a change of heart," a man said, stepping from the shadows. "And after all the trouble I went through to locate this...costume."

Jenny recognized the stranger's voice, how could she not when it glided over the syllables so beautifully, but what in the world was he talking about? What costume? And *dearest*?

"Hold on now, who are ye? What do ye mean by trespassin' here?" the guard holding her arm shouted.

"Apologies, my good man, but the lady is a bit of a romantic, and wanting to please her...well, you understand."

Confusion, a very uncomfortable state of being for Jenny, clouded her mind. The man was either insane or trying to charm his way out of this mess, but to what end and what role did she play in his odd game?

The other guard appeared and snagged the stranger's arm. "You ain't goin' nowhere, boyo."

"I have no intention of leaving. Not without the lady."

He could be an accomplice to the kidnapper who tried to grab her last summer in this very garden, she reasoned. But if so, why wait until now to make another attempt?

Well, Tuck was a rather formidable guard. He could've been following them for some time waiting for the moment when Jenny would be alone. But Tuck would've known he was there. She had an uncanny knack for subterfuge in all forms. And then again, her friend had been rather consumed with her need to get back to Colin in the sixteenth century.

Numerous hypotheses filtered through Jenny's thoughts and were properly cataloged, but none of them held as much appeal as the stranger.

Appeal? Good grief. This incident had affected her cognitive abilities. The fact that the man was wonderfully fit—a fact she'd deduced as he'd held her—and possessed a delicious English accent laced with seduction, had managed to blur her judgment. She was, as he so

9

eloquently stated, a romantic. Tuck teased her on many occasions about being a Cinderella-wannabe in a world where there were no Prince Charmings.

She sighed. Well, at least she couldn't see the man without her glasses. If he looked like he sounded and felt, she would be in major trouble. Swooning over a would-be kidnapper was not the wisest of things to add to her list of accomplishments. And dwelling on the man and her array of hypotheses was not going to get her out of this mess. What she needed was a friend. One with fighting skills and a quick mind. The only person who could get her out of anything.

"Tuck, I could really use your help right now," she murmured, but knew her friend was long gone.

"Tuck, is it? Well, Tuck, ye and the misses are about tae have a chat with the constable," the guard said.

"I am afraid you are mistaken. My name is not Tuck." With a courtly bow, the stranger said, "Ian Southernland, at your service."

Jenny gasped then squinted hard in a vain attempt to see him. It wasn't possible. This couldn't be Tuck's friend from the past. This wasn't one of her hypotheses. Ian Southernland wasn't even in the blasted equation!

"Hooo, fancy mon, fancy clothes," the guard beside him said. "Are ye supposed tae be some sort of lord?" he asked with a chuckle.

"My rank is of no consequence. However, to set the matter straight, I am a fourth son of a baron. Not a lord."

"Another loonie," the other guard grumbled.

"Nay, my good man. Not a loonie, nor a nutball, but a man in love."

Both guards laughed, while Jenny could do nothing but blink. *Love?* He had to be insane. And as to claiming he was Ian Southernland, she and Tuck must have said something out loud. It was the only reasonable explanation.

The stranger stepped forward and took her hand, easing her from the guard's grasp, and placed a kiss against the back. The warmth of his breath slid beneath the cuff of her coat and traveled up her arm then enveloped her entire body.

She shook her head at the absolute nonsense racing

through her brain. A combination of too much fantasy, the cold night air, the disquieting situation of being caught trespassing on private property, seeing her friend disappear through a time portal, and a flux in her pheromone level, was causing her body temperature to rise and her cheeks to flush. Yes, that was it. Completely logical. It had nothing to do with the man in front of her. Nothing at all.

That conundrum solved, left the question of this man's true identity and purpose. Up close and squinting, she could see some of his costume, sort of, and noted its authenticity in the dim light, but he couldn't be Ian Southernland. Her theory of time travel through this particular portal—having not ruled out the possible existence of others—should have placed him in the twenty-first century on an equinox, not a solstice, ergo he could not be Ian Southernland. He had to have been watching her and Tuck for some time, listening to their conversations without them knowing.

"Ye mean tae tell me, ye dressed up like that, stole onto private property in the middle of the night, a blasted freezin' one at that, and all tae please a woman?" The guard let out a hearty chuckle. "And ye doona think that's daft?"

Ian slipped his arm around Jenny's waist. She tried to refrain from any reactionary display, but her body trembled in response to the contact. A man hadn't touched her like this in years. Her own fault really, her work took up most if not all of her time, it was all she had. It was the only thing that granted her some attention from her father.

Her chin dropped at the thought. She hadn't realized how pathetic she'd become over the years, doing anything to gain his attention. More importantly why would such a revelation come to her now? This was not the time to dwell on such things.

She jerked her wandering mind back to the problem at hand. A lunatic had a firm hold of her waist, and she found she was not inclined to move away. Maybe she was the one insane.

"A classic tale, my friend. A man in love is oft' misunderstood," the stranger said, then gently stroked her cheek. "Yet, how can you not understand when the lady is so lovely?"

Lovely? Oh, Jenny wished the guard would shine the light on him so she could see at least something instead of a shadowy, blurry silhouette.

You silly, juvenile, ridiculous—it doesn't matter that Tuck described him as Prince Charming, or that you dreamed he was your Prince Charming. He is just a man, who doesn't want you, regardless of what he's saying now. It's all for—for, why is he saying these ridiculous things? Who is he really?

"Gentleman, let us take this discussion inside where we might warm ourselves, and I will be happy to tell you the entire tale while we await the constable," the stranger said, easing them all toward the castle.

With a chuckle the guards flanked them and walked alongside.

"You can't be Ian. It isn't possible," she whispered, determined to get some of the puzzle sorted out, hoping to bring this person to his senses. Before she lost hers.

"Aye, but it is possible, mistress. Amelia sent me to fetch you."

"She only just left. The fountain doesn't—" She bit off her words. Telling this man or anyone else about the time portal would be a monumental mistake. Even though she suspected he already knew too much.

"I have a theory about this unusual form of travel you have discovered," he said lowly.

She swallowed hard. "I don't know what you're talking about."

Ian chuckled. "You are a sad liar, little one. You know of what I speak."

Jenny attempted to wriggle out of his grasp without drawing the guards' attention, but had little luck. He merely tightened his hold, and blast her fickle body, she liked it!

"Even if I did, I'm not about to discuss theories of any sort with a person lying about his identity," she said, straightening her shoulders. "Besides, the complexities of temporal mechanics or the possible existence of a time anomaly along with the massive implications would be beyond your comprehension."

He stopped in mid-stride, releasing her. "I know more than you might think having experienced the *anomaly* first hand," he said, clearly annoyed.

She returned his steady gaze, although for her he was but a dark, indistinct figure. Still, a debate was at hand, not a very challenging one considering the man was, after all, claiming to be a sixteenth century Englishman, but it was a debate nonetheless.

"You hold but a few seemingly interesting facts that you gained from eavesdropping, and something you *think* you witnessed," she said, deducing that he had to have seen Tuck disappear. "Along with some recent study of my background and Tuck's as well. But you cannot possibly have any real information that would bring you to a logical conclusion pertaining to the current situation." She reached to straighten her glasses, and cursed softly at their absence. A bad habit of hers, she knew, but more annoying with their disappearance.

"Now, now, you two. No lover's spats," the portly guard said with a boisterous laugh, his friend laughing with him.

"The current situation is that you, Mistress Maxwell, are a woman," the man said. "And women are well known for allowing their emotions to interfere with clear thinking. With the occurrences of this evening, my very presence having unnerved you, it is highly likely *that* is the case."

Nothing but a squeak of indignation passed her lips. No one, not even her father, had ever questioned her intelligence. Ever!

"Now if you do not mind, I would very much like to complete my task and return home," he said, taking a firm hold of her hand and started walking once again.

"And what would that task be?" she asked, falling instep beside him, although she had no choice. "Hold me hostage for ransom? My father won't pay you."

Ian slowed his stride, struck by the faint fear behind her voice. He damned himself for letting his own temper get away with him. The entire situation, this time travel nonsense had muddled his thinking. This woman had previously been attacked, Amelia had told him of the tale, and here he was trying to carry her off without fully explaining himself. Not only had he yet to convince her of his identity, his charm did not appear to work on this woman. Although he had to admit, he'd not had ample opportunity to win her favor.

A trickling and splashing of water reached Ian's ears, and he knew they were close to the fountain. Rounding the last hedgerow, his eyes lit on the sight that would take him home. The pale moonlight glinted off the water, sparkling like the very stars in the sky. Now was his moment...their moment.

"Gentleman, I have a request, if you please, before we go inside." He paused beside the fountain, Jenny's hand still firmly in his. "This, you see," he said motioning to the fountain, "was where we had planned to meet. So, if you would be so kind as to indulge me for a brief moment, then this journey will not be a complete loss."

He looked at the young miss and her wide, startled gaze. "I am whom I say I am, mistress. Amelia and Colin did send me. They need you, Jenny Maxwell. Do not doubt what your eyes and heart tell you."

Her mouth fell open and she cast a startled glance at the fountain. Ian did not blame her for her trepidation, the trip was a bit nauseating, and one was not completely certain *when* one would land.

"Oh, let the man. What harm is there?" one of the guard's blustered.

"Aye, Errol. It might be a good show," he said with a chuckle. "Have at it, mon."

"Aye, a very good show, I dare say," Ian murmured. "The time has come for you and I to take a step into a different world," he said, clasping Jenny's hand to his chest. "One far different from this one. I made a vow to take you there. One I cannot break. Now is the time for your decision. Do I travel alone or will you accompany me?"

One of the guards cleared his throat, a distinct laugh behind it. "No offense, mon, but that has tae be the worst proposal I've ever heard."

"I—I don't know. I—are you really Ian?" she whispered, her voice a tad shaky to his ears.

"Aye, mistress. 'Tis the truth. The time grows late," he said, nodding toward the rising sun. "Your answer, if you please."

She rubbed her brow. "I don't know. I don't understand how you could've come forward," she whispered. "Nor how you could go back on the same night. And even if you—*we* do, the consequences of what might happen, the things that might be changed because of me..." She nodded toward the sentries. "And the things they'll tell people. As much as I want to go, I can't chance it."

"'Tis worth the risk, mistress. Your friend, our friends need you."

"Och, kiss her ye dolt," the guard called and the other laughed in agreement.

'Twas tempting, Ian thought. Especially considering he had not kissed a maid in an age. But alas, now was not the time.

"M-my father needs me," she stammered over the words and licked her lips. They glistened in the faint light, a most appealing sight.

Perhaps words were not what the situation called for after all. He slid his hand to the back of her neck and pulled her into his arms for a searing kiss, one that brook no argument, and none did he receive.

She melted against him on a sigh and he stole into her mouth and the sheer heaven of her heat. Aye, he had been without a woman in his arms for far too long. But he needed to move on, and not, unfortunately, toward an inviting bed.

He scooped her up and leaped onto the edge of the fountain, regretting the abrupt end to the kiss. There was a small flame burning within this petite female begging to be encouraged, and he would very much like to be the one to accommodate her.

"What are you doing?" she demanded, although her voice was weak at best.

"Gentleman, I ask you. Do you believe in...ghosts?" Ian stepped into the fountain with a reluctant passenger in his arms, and faded into the last slip of night leaving nothing but a haunting laugh in his wake.

"Errol, do ye still have that scotch hidden in the bottom of yer desk?" the guard asked with a harsh swallow.

"Aye."

With that the two men turned from the fountain, both vowing never to say a word to a soul.

Chapter Two

"Oh, my head," Mistress Maxwell groaned.

"Aye, 'tis a bit nauseating, but one grows accustomed to it," Ian said.

"But the castle—the gardens—"

"Have not yet been built."

"Then we—"

"Aye, mistress. We did," he said, rather smugly, but the woman was a bit of a curmudgeon. It felt good to have proven his claim.

"Would you please quit finishing my sentences? And who do you think you are? You can't just grab a woman like that and—and—"

"Kiss her?" he asked with a chuckle. He really had enjoyed that, but considering the current situation, he doubted he would ever get another from the young lady. A gentleman did not seduce his friends' guests, well not in this case, at least. This particular guest was not staying, and he had the distinct feeling his advances would not be welcome. Although she did seem to have enjoyed the exchange as much as he.

"I was going to say, step into time portals," she snarled. "Weren't you listening to me? Have you any idea what you've done? The risk involved, and those men—"

"Those men will say nary a word about what they believe they saw," he said, striding across the small clearing still carrying his burden, although there was little to her.

"Who are you to decide the track of history? They could very easily try to follow us."

"Nonsense."

"Of all the—" She sighed, tickling the side of his neck with her breath. Rather pleasant, but he forced himself to ignore it as it would do him no good.

"You must try to understand," she said. "I know that

17

the concept of time travel, although you've experienced it first hand, can be a bit difficult to comprehend, but your rash behavior could very well have changed history."

Ian clenched his teeth and stopped, his eyes shut tight. "Mistress. Your incessant need to slight my intelligence is proving tiresome. I suggest you do not make the mistake again, or I shall quite happily drop you here upon this soggy patch of earth and let you find your way to Arreyder Castle alone."

"I merely made a logical deduction that your comprehension of time travel would be highly limited based upon the period in which you were born. Your education would never have touched on a topic so radical that anyone discussing it would likely have been accused of heresy."

"Aye. I understand so little that I have brought you back through time, a portal you were convinced would not function, to mere seconds after I left."

"That can't be right. It simply doesn't equate."

"'Tis correct, regardless of your way of thinking. The truth is around you, if you would but look. Your time portal does not attach itself to any one person, but has a schedule of its own."

"If you left on a summer solstice and arrived on a winter solstice—"

"I was merely completing the trip that Amelia had begun."

She fell silent for a moment, and he hoped 'twould be the end of the discussion, but alas, it was not.

"Interesting, but how do you explain our arrival in the correct time? If this is the correct time. We should have started a new loop. No, I'm sorry, your theory can't be correct."

With a weighty sigh, Ian continued across the clearing toward Colin where he stood with a large smile on his face. All the while the woman-child in his arms continued her babbling about the many holes in his theory, while completely avoiding the holes in her own.

Although kissing her had been most pleasant, her remarks toward him were disturbing, and far too familiar. His own father had said things along the same vein many times. Never directly insulting him or his intelligence, but always hinting that he was an imbecile. One of the many reasons he had not ventured onto his father's estate in ten years.

"Did you have to steal the woman, mon? Did your charm no' have her falling at your feet?" Colin asked with a boisterous laugh, pulling him from his thoughts.

The woman fell silent and still in his arms. Ian dared a look in her direction, wondering if she'd simply worn herself out with all her talking. But she was quite awake, he discovered, and not at all what he'd thought he'd seen in the flash of the sentry's light across her features.

Framing an impish face, deep brown hair that caught the summer sun and held it captive lay across her breast bound in a tight braid. He actually ached to feel the silkiness once again against his cheek. Her head turned and when she looked at him, her bow shaped mouth open in surprise, he fell quite haplessly into the largest pair of brown eyes it had ever been his pleasure to view.

Her form was slight, aye, but a woman's form. He experienced her pleasing shape firsthand, as she lay cradled in his arms. Her delicate, fey-like features, however, were what captured his complete attention. She was, quite simply, the fairest female he had ever seen.

"You mean tae tell me this wee thing is the physician Amelia has gone on about? The scientist?" Colin asked.

Ian pulled his gaze from the disquieting woman and cleared his constricted throat. "Aye. Jenny Maxwell, may I present Colin MacLean."

"I—I—" Ian watched her long delicate throat move as she swallowed. "It's nice to meet you," she said, her voice all but a whisper.

Colin shook his head with a chuckle. "I'll ne'er understand the future, and glad that I am Amelia wishes tae live here. But I'm happy you've come, lass. 'Twill make Amelia happy and 'tis all that matters tae me."

He turned toward the horses and Ian followed. He never once thought to put the lady down, it simply didn't occur to him.

Nearing his mount, she gasped.

"Is something amiss?" he asked.

Jenny squinted, trying to dismiss what she knew she was seeing. *Horses. Wonderful.* Not only had she never ridden, she was petrified at the very thought of such an endeavor.

"Are you not well?" Ian asked. She refrained from clinging to him in terror.

"I'd rather walk, if you don't mind," she said.

"The lady wishes to walk," he called to Colin.

The large Scot grumbled, but she heard a 'so be it' from his general vicinity. She really wished she hadn't lost her glasses. She could barely distinguish the men from the horses. Well, except for the fact that Ian still held her. It felt awfully nice, but was about to end, and of course he would have no need to pick her up again. Or kiss her again.

She stored the feel of his arms around her in the back of her mind as well as that kiss. Dwelling on it now wouldn't do her any good. According to Tuck's description of the man, he was a regular rogue, a ladies' man, and not likely to be interested in her. No one was interested in her, her brain at times, but never her.

Slowly her feet touched the ground and the warmth and security from his arms disappeared. She withheld her sigh of pleasure and regret.

"The castle is this way," Ian said and she fell in step beside him, thankful he was kind enough to lead his horse rather than ride.

Colin rode on ahead a few yards. He was exactly as expected, a very large, gruff Scot full of bluster. She smiled, knowing Tuck had found the man for her.

Jenny's thoughts shifted to the man beside her then abruptly back to Raghnall Castle. She prayed the night-guards wouldn't follow them, or worse find a path to a different time and radically change history.

****

A keen eye observed from a copse of trees nearby. Although a little shaken by his ride through time, Vernon Cox was not one to let anything or anyone get the better of him. Not even a mousy scientist by the name of Jenny Maxwell. But he'd been so close!

He'd watched her for months since that idiot had blown it last summer. At least he'd made the deal with the thug he'd hired anonymously. He couldn't identify him. But that left Vernon to handle the thing himself.

He'd followed her and that bodyguard all over Europe. Pacing himself, waiting for just the right moment. Then it came.

She'd been left alone at Raghnall Castle after her bodyguard stepped into the fountain and vanished. There was nothing to stop him. Although, the woman's disappearance had peaked his interest, he didn't have time to explore it. He had to grab the brat and extract his revenge on her father. That was his top priority. Nothing would detract him from his course. But then that moronic Englishman showed up and ruined everything! Between him and those two bumbling guards at the castle, he'd missed his chance. But it wouldn't be his last.

Vernon followed Jenny closely, he wasn't about to lose sight of her. Not when he'd come so close. "You'll get yours too, Englishman," he murmured. No one outwitted Vernon Cox. No one.

Her father may think he'd succeeded, but he would soon be proved wrong. Richard Maxwell wouldn't be earning millions on his discovery for much longer. He should've known Maxwell was a cheat and a liar. Stealing was easier than inventing. But he would have his revenge and his recognition, and kidnapping Jenny Maxwell was the best way. With her in his hands, he could bargain with her father, trade her life for full recognition of his discovery.

But he was no fool. He knew he'd go to prison for what he was doing, but the world would know he was the creator of EQ13. Not Maxwell industries. Not Maxwell's daughter. Vernon Cox was the genius! Vernon Cox was the greatest scientist of all time!

And now, he thought with a smile, with the portal at his disposal he could avoid incarceration. He would have to thank Jenny Maxwell for that little piece of information, and he would when the time was right. His fingers brushed against the gun shoved in his belt.

The brat stumbled and the English idiot caught her by the arm.

"Thanks," Jenny mumbled, she really was lost without her glasses.

"'Twould be much simpler if we were to ride," Ian said.

"No, no. I'm fine. Really. It's—uh—it's a lovely day for a walk."

"'Tis a trek to the castle, one I wager will leave you quite winded, little one."

She shot him a look at the nickname, at least she think she did. That could've been the horse she was looking at, she couldn't be certain, but she did despise the name he'd given her. It sounded as if she were a child and not a grown woman. Not unlike the feeling she got when her father was fuming at her. She always felt so small then.

Another hateful stone or branch or something tripped her again. This time Ian's arm came around her waist and pressed her back against his broad chest.

"You, my dear lady, are not of a mind to watch your step."

"A little difficult since I lost my glasses when I ran into the guard." She smirked at him over her shoulder. "When I was running from you."

He chuckled softly, sending a faint quiver down her spine. "You cannot blame your impairment on me, little one."

"I most certainly can. And stop calling me that. If you had explained who you were in the beginning, I wouldn't have run into the guard and lost my glasses. My current predicament is a direct result of your poor planning."

"Really? I thought it rather ingenious myself," he said.

Jenny blew at a stray tendril tickling her cheek. "Well, your ingenious plan has left me practically blind. It would've been better to have stayed until the next portal opening so that I could've gathered any number of items that would make my visit here more productive and safe."

"Are you two going tae stand around all day? My wife isna a patient lass," Colin called back to them.

"You just wish to get back to her," Ian said with a laugh, warm and rich. "A more besotted Scot I have ne'er seen. Go on ahead, and we shall be along in a thrice."

Colin chuckled. "Aye, now there's a grand idea."

The horse took off leaving a trail of dust behind. Jenny couldn't help but smile...on the outside. On the inside she was jealous. To have a man love her that much would be the greatest gift.

"Now, mistress. 'Tis time to make haste," Ian said, his hold on her tightening just before he lifted her off her feet.

"What is this propensity you have with picking me up?"

"'Tis logical," he said with a chuckle. "You are small. I am big. I wish to get to the castle quickly and cannot leave you behind to find your way."

"You said you'd leave me in the clearing."

"Aye, that I did. But I have now come to realize that Colin would have my head if I were to do so. Ergo, we ride."

She squeaked as he climbed aboard his massive horse with her in his arms, her lids clamped closed while she held on with all her might.

"I shall not drop you," he said softly in her ear. She relaxed a smidgeon, her mind quickly running away with that wonderful voice of his, dreaming of other things he might say and what he'd be doing when he said them.

Then the horse moved.

He chuckled as she clutched at him. "Drake is a gentle animal, he will not harm you. You are quite safe."

"You're sure?"

"I gather you have ne'er sat upon a horse before."

"No. Terrified of them, to be exact," she said, with a faint shake of her head, as she buried her face deeper into his doublet.

Ian shifted in his saddle somewhat, surprised by his reaction to the woman. They did not get on well, although he liked her form and face, her temperament left much to be desired. But for her to openly admit her fear was a brave thing. And yet to be afraid of horses was unfathomable to him. The beasts had always held a fascination for Ian, their beauty, their grace, their strength...aye, other men's horseflesh could prove difficult at times, but not his.

Determined to sway her fear as much as possible, he said, "You are safe, I swear it on my life. I will not let anything happen to you." He dismissed the fierce protective tone his voice had taken and cleared his throat. "Open your eyes or you shall miss your first glimpse of

Arreyder Castle in my time."

"You know I can't see. Not really," she muttered against his chest.

"'Tis that bad, truly?"

"Yes. I'm extremely myopic. That means—"

"I know what myopic means."

"Oh. Um, well, my case is bad enough that I have to be within a foot of something to see it, and even then not all that well."

Ian resisted the urge to stroke her long braid dancing over her shoulder as they left the trees and approached the castle. Perhaps she was right, perhaps he had made a rash decision by returning so soon. How could she aid Amelia when she could not see?

"How much farther?" she asked.

"Not far. Bleary-eyed or no, would you not care to see?"

He watched as she tentatively opened her eyes and peered about, her grip on his doublet, however did not lighten.

She squinted, quite charmingly then frowned. "No, I'm afraid I can't see anything. The castle is intact in my time so I doubt there would be that much difference. There's a road, a parking lot, some shops, and loads of tourists, but no villagers."

"No villagers? Who plants the crops, tends the fields and cattle?"

"No one. The lands are managed in other ways in my time."

She went on to expound on the economic structure of Scotland in her time, thoroughly fascinating Ian. Amelia had many a marvelous tale to tell, but hers were of exploits, adventures, and the like around the world. This was minute detail he could never have hoped to gleam from his lady friend.

"I'm sorry. You probably don't understand most of what I'm talking about," she said.

He sighed at her slight and focused on the castle. "You would be surprised what I understand."

"I've insulted you again, haven't I?"

"You have a talent for it, aye." It was growing more difficult with the passing days and his stay at Arreyder to keep his memories, his failings to himself. What with Colin's marriage, there was naught else to occupy his time or his mind.

"Sorry. I do it to everyone. I think Tuck is the only person that I don't make feel that way when I fall into lecture mode. She has the ability to gleam what she needs to know from my dissertations and without being insulted or bored. At least she isn't visibly bored. Another talent she has, hiding her emotions beneath a stony façade."

Ian studied her from the corner of his eye. What an odd little bird she was. An extremely intelligent mind existed in this petite woman. A woman who felt things deeply, he sensed it was so. Her talk of Amelia and her many talents gave away her devout loyalty and love for her friend. But she knew little of what people hid behind their false smiles. His own included.

"I understand, mistress."

"You do?"

"Aye, I am oft' misunderstood, but not for my speech." Because of his handsome visage, his propensity to charm, and his popularity with women, many saw him as an empty-headed rogue, the role he'd been destined to play since birth. But in truth he had knowledge of many things, and a deep desire to know more, to explore the world around him.

"Amelia does not hide her feelings, of late, however," he said, changing the avenue of his thoughts.

"Oh?"

"You shall see soon enough."

"Easier said than done," she murmured, niggling his conscience just a bit.

"We have arrived," Ian said, and climbed down from his horse with her in his arms then placed her on her feet. One of Colin's men took his horse, but not before shooting Jenny an interested look.

Before Ian could set the lad straight, that this was a lady and not a woman to trifle with, a gangly Amelia toddled out the door and enveloped the woman in a hug. "Jenny! I can't believe you're here," she said, bursting into tears.

"Tuck?" Jenny said, putting a little distance between them. She peered at her friend, her large brown eyes taking in as much as they could without her spectacles. "It's so good to see you, all of you—sort of."

"Oh, your glasses. Oh no. Ian what did you do?" Amelia said, her hands fisted at her hips.

"I?"

"Yes you. She needs her glasses. How could you lose them?"

"I did not! She ran and—"

"Ran?" Amelia blinked at him, her mouth twisting. "From you? From Prince Charming?" A laugh, quite uncalled for, burst forth.

"'Twas dark when I arrived," he snarled, knowing all too well he would be the center of her jest for some time.

"Wait, did you say dark?" Amelia asked.

"Aye, dark. As in night."

"But you couldn't have arrived at night. Even I didn't when I came back." Amelia sighed and rubbed her forehead. "I don't understand. What exactly happened when you left here? Be specific."

"Yes, please. Be very specific," the small woman by her side said, her large brown eyes narrowed, her arms folded over her breasts as she looked at him.

With a sigh he began. "I arrived on the night you left, Amelia. Mere moments after, 'twould be my guess." Both women shook their heads, but he continued, cutting off their disagreement. "'Twould appear that I was completing the trip you began when you returned here last autumn." He crossed his arms and returned the young maid's direct scrutiny.

"But that negates the second part of your theory," Jenny argued. "You started a new loop when you grabbed me, and as I've said before, we wouldn't have landed here at this time."

He leaned close to her so she would clearly see him, or thereabouts. "And yet here we stand. You are simply too stubborn to accept the fact that your theory is incorrect."

"And you refuse to see that your theory is nothing more than speculation based on one incident."

"And yours is based on what? A pair of incidents? How does that liken to a more logical conclusion?"

Amelia and Colin exchanged amused glances as the

two continued their heated debate. "Do you suppose they'd notice if we went inside?" Amelia asked her husband.

"I doona think they have even noticed the rain, love," Colin said with a chuckle. "Come. Let us get you and my son—or daughter," he corrected with a grin before she could swat him, "where 'tis warm and dry. They'll be along in a bit." Colin escorted his wife through the door. "Sadly, it looks as if the lass was caught unaware."

Amelia chuckled. "Sorry, Colin. You'll just have to do without a new supply of Gummy Bears."

"Och, more's the pity," he said with a grin.

"You doona mean tae say you're going tae leave them out in this?" Colin's Aunt Elspeth sputtered.

Colin and Amelia shrugged, then paused inside the entrance as Elspeth took the matter fully in hand. "Ian Southernland, that is quite enough. Escort the young lass inside before she catches her death," she called out.

Ian blinked once, then twice, then realized his rather wet surroundings. The petite woman had a head as hard as Amelia's, her continued arguing was proof of that, and in the rain no less. But she did not possess the stamina. She was a small thing, not a female soldier like Amelia. Elspeth was correct, she should be inside where it was warm.

Ian set aside their rather interesting debate, although it was a bit irrational, but she was a woman after all. Without another thought, he scooped her up and trotted up the stairs into the main hall with Elspeth fussing alongside him.

"Why is it, that whenever you're losing an argument you pick me up?" Jenny asked with a soft growl. One he rather liked, blast his libidinous self.

"It seemed the most expeditious way in which to get dry," he said, determined to douse his inconvenient and inappropriate desires. "And I was not losing."

"You were most definitely losing. If you would only see—"

"Children, please," Elspeth said with a heavy sigh. "Ian you may place the lass on her feet."

Ian did as Elspeth bade him, but with some reluctance. He was discovering he sorely enjoyed the feel of the petite maid in his arms, almost as much as their heated debate. The woman stirred something in him he'd not known existed. Perhaps there was more than pleasure he was in need of. Or perhaps he had lost his mind entirely.

"Now, lass, I'll take you tae your room where you can dry yourself and have a wee rest," Elspeth said.

"Oh, well, thank you, but I'd much rather see to Tuck right now, if you don't mind." Jenny turned in the direction of her friend. "I assume you wanted me here for the baby's sake, am I right?"

Tuck laughed. "Even without your glasses you could tell, huh? I know, I'm as big as a Panzer, but yeah. I wanted you here to make sure it all goes well. Not that Elspeth isn't perfectly capable of handling things," she said quickly with a smile toward her aunt. "I just wanted—I just thought—"

"I understand. I just hope that I can be of help without my glasses or any supplies," she said, shooting Ian a look.

"'Twas not my fault you lost your bloody spectacles," he growled.

"Perhaps, but my instruments would've been extremely beneficial. If only you'd allowed me to—"

"There was no time to fetch your instruments."

"There would've been if you'd explained yourself in the first place."

"I tried, you ran."

"You grabbed me!"

"You would have been caught!"

"Children!" They fell silent at Elspeth bark, but neither moved, once again toe to toe.

"Och, you two are a pair," Elspeth said with a sigh. "Now, lass, we'll go tae your chamber while Colin helps Amelia tae theirs. You've got tae get out of those wet things, at least. And you need tae dry yourself, lad. Off with you," she said, shooing Ian away.

"Go ahead, Jenny. It takes me a long time to get to my room. This bus has only one gear, low," Amelia said with a snort. "And I do have a few medical supplies, remember?"

"Oh yes, I'd forgotten. They'll help, but I'm sure you

didn't pack an extra pair of glasses for me." That last comment was aimed at him, Ian was certain.

Elspeth took Jenny's arm and guided her up the stairs with Amelia slowly moving along behind.

"Bloody spectacles," Ian grumbled, stomping along behind them toward his chamber.

Chapter Three

Jenny could barely believe it. Tuck blubbering on her shoulder and as huge as a house? It seemed unreal. Well then, so did time travel, so she supposed it fit into the scheme of things. Her big bad bodyguard was going to be a mother. It was the last thing Jenny had ever expected. She hadn't time during her brief journey to contemplate why Colin and Tuck would've sent Ian to get her. There were too many other variables involved in her situation to allow her a moment to turn her attention to that puzzle.

Like a strong man with a hypnotic voice and heavenly lips?

She silently chastised herself for letting her thoughts run amok. There were other things to think on, like Tuck's child. Men were not in the equation. And there were so many other things to consider.

Mostly, she realized as she ran her hand over the homespun dress she wore, she was in sixteenth century Scotland. She was living a dream, she was experiencing a great adventure. The reality of it all had her perching on the edge of the bed, her knees a bit weak.

Never had she ever guessed where her association with Amelia Tucker would take her. Locked away in her lab for most of her adult years, she'd never imagined she would have such exploits. Her father's insistence that she take a trip to Europe had led to the most amazing adventure of all. She'd been beyond jealous of Tuck and her trip through time, but was too much a coward to take the trip herself. But Ian Southernland had left her no choice.

She moaned and rubbed her forehead. With luck, the bedpost won't have left a mark where she plowed into it earlier. But that wasn't the cause of her headache. She had to thank the pigheaded Englishman who brought her here, but it galled her to do it.

There was a knock at the door. "Jenny dear, are you ready?" Elspeth called.

"Yes." She stood and watched a blurry round woman come into the room. Elspeth took her hand and led her safely past the bed, through the door, and down the hall.

"Elspeth, I'll need you to be my eyes while I examine Tuck."

"Of course dear," she said, and patted her hand. "I'm not sure what you've seen thus far, but Amelia is very large. I have no' seen anyone so big with child afore."

"Really? Interesting. How far along is she?"

"She's only in her seventh month, I'm thinkin', but 'twould seem closer tae her ninth if you but look at her." She sighed. "Tae believe I am about tae become a grandmother and a great aunt at the same time. I have been truly blessed."

"Yes, you have," she murmured, recalling that Elspeth had wed Colin's father during Tuck's first visit.

She cleared her throat, dissolving the jealousy rising inside her. Was she doomed to be alone, not wanted, with no family of her own her entire life? Even her father's insistence that she take a tour of Europe was mostly to get her out of his hair after her completion of her tests on EQ13.

He'd placed high hopes that it would make him *more* millions. But as she surmised, the drug was only a passing success, nothing too earth shattering and definitely not worth millions. So he sent her away, told her it was for her own good, when she knew it was because he couldn't stand the sight of her. Even the kidnapping threats hadn't stopped him from pushing her out. At least he'd assigned Tuck as her bodyguard.

The thought of her bodyguard-turned-friend brought a smile to her face. Tuck was her only friend. One who wanted her here to help her with her pregnancy, but not just because she was a doctor. Tuck trusted her, cared about her. That was something Jenny couldn't ignore. What a shame she had to live in a different time. It put a major damper on visits, and yet here she was.

"Do you suppose 'tis the fare I've been giving her that's made her so big?" Elspeth asked, pulling Jenny from her thoughts.

"I doubt it. She wouldn't eat unless she was hungry and, well, both Tuck and Colin are big people, so a large baby isn't surprising."

Elspeth chuckled. "Aye, that they are. Glad, I'll be when you've had a look at the lass."

Jenny cringed. How could she possibly be of any use without her glasses?

"Here we are," Elspeth said as she led Jenny into Tuck's room.

"Finally! I can't wait to hear what you've got to say," Tuck said, her voice tight with worry as she shoved the bag of medical supplies into her hands.

"I'm sure you're fine. Isn't that right, Elspeth?"

"Aye, tae be sure. Now, Colin, this is woman's work. Off with you."

"I'll no' be leavin' at a time like this."

Jenny laughed softly, wishing for the hundredth time that someone might care for her that much. "It's okay, Elspeth. Without my glasses, the sort of checkup I'm going to give her won't be very invasive. There isn't any point, since I won't be able to see what I need to see."

"I will leave for Edinburgh on the morrow," Ian said as he strolled into the room. "There I shall acquire you a new pair of spectacles," he said with finality.

Jenny held in the shiver his voice caused. "You won't be able to find any. Not in this century. Not like the ones I require," she said, refusing to look at him. His impressive height and size were all quite visible, and she knew how it felt to be held against his massive chest. Not looking would help her to not want, or so she theorized.

"I will find you a pair of spectacles. For the most severe myopia 'twas e'er seen."

"You mean for someone blind as a bat," she snipped, jerking the stethoscope from the bag then clipping it around her neck.

"'Twas not what I said."

Turning to face this irritant, she fisted her hands at her hips. "You still can't choose them for me. It would be a waste of time."

He stepped closer, towering over her. "I can and I will."

"You won't."

"I say you need the bloody things and I *will* get them!"

"And I say you won't get anything but a piece of worthless glass!"

"Colin, do me a favor," Amelia said. "Grab him and get out of here so I can have my physical. Before I kill both of them."

With a chuckle, Colin kissed her, then snagged Ian by the collar.

"Bloody termagant," Ian bellowed as he was hauled backward.

"Obstinate ass!"

The door slammed soundly ending the argument.

"Well," Elspeth said. "Now that that's settled, let us see tae my grandchild, shall we?"

****

"Did you hear what she called me?" Ian sputtered.

Colin chuckled heartily. "I think the lass has spirit."

"Spirit? She is a-a-bloody lunatic! Regardless of the facts presented before her, she is determined to disagree with them, merely because I am the bearer of such information. I shall grant you she is intelligent, but never a more hard-headed woman has it e'er been my *dis*pleasure to meet."

"Like her that much, do you?"

"That 'tis a very poor jest, my friend."

"But an apt one, eh? Do you no' remember how Amelia and I were at crossed swords in the beginning? 'Tis the first woman you have e'er met, other than my Amelia, that meets you head on as a man instead of swooning at that pretty face of yours. And you, my friend, doona know what tae do about it." He slapped him on the back. "That annoying charm of yours willna' help you this time."

"As usual, you have lost what little brain you were gifted with upon your birth. That female is not for me," he protested, but Colin only grinned wider. "'Tis inconceivable!"

"The woman is tiny aye, but a very pretty lass she is. And you canna lie tae save your soul, Sassenach, so doona try."

"I ne'er said she was not pretty." He adjusted his

33

doublet from Colin's handling. "She is quite comely. Until she opens her mouth." Unless he was kissing her, then her mouth was quite a joy.

Colin laughed heartily. "'Tis such a good turn tae see you suffer as I suffered."

"Delusional, as usual. You are imagining things. Seeing things that are not there through those lovesick eyes of yours. Either that or the fact you are about to become a father has stolen the last bit of sense you e'er had."

Colin sobered. "A father. I still canna believe it." He leaned against the wall and stared at the closed door before them. "What do you suppose is takin' so bleedin' long?"

Ian relaxed and took a place beside him against the wall. "We shall no doubt know something soon enough."

Ian worried for Amelia, but his friend's previous observations were what plagued his mind. They were entirely too accurate. Yes, he liked the woman, far more than he liked any other, and yet he could not fathom why. She was stubborn, hardheaded, and argumentative. They were at odds over nearly every topic thus far. And she was a tiny thing, when he was a rather large figure of a man. He'd always leaned toward those women who were hardier than Jenny Maxwell. One of the many reasons he'd hoped, although only idly, to court Amelia when they'd first met. But it wasn't long before she fell quite hopelessly in love with his friend.

But this woman. No, the idea was ridiculous. He admitted that her fey-like features and delicate form were enticing, but she was not for him. He stroked his chin. That kiss however...

The door opened, thankfully interrupting the direction of his thoughts. Colin braced himself, no doubt afraid of the worst. Ian gripped his shoulder, offering his support in whatever was to come.

Elspeth's smiling face peaked out and motioned them inside.

Colin rushed to Amelia's side where she lay upon the bed, her face awash with tears. "Mavourneen, what ails you?"

Ian stole a glance at Jenny as she took the

stethoscope, he believed 'twas called, from her ears. She sported a bright smile. Whatever the cause of Amelia's tears, they were happy ones, thank heaven.

"We—we're—" Amelia blubbered and loudly. A sight Ian would ne'er get used to, but since the babe, she seemed to do so often.

"What is it? Tell me what's wrong," Colin demanded of Jenny, his face contorted with worry.

"You're going to be the father of twins," Jenny said, still smiling. She was quite lovely. And although Ian felt the weight lift off his shoulders at the good news, he couldn't help but notice a faint sadness in Jenny's eyes.

"Twins?" Colin squeaked, not a manly sound, but considering the news, Ian could not fault him for it.

"Everyone is quite healthy and I expect a somewhat easy delivery, considering things, but she is confined to bed for the duration," Jenny said.

"Hell," Amelia grumbled with the last of her sniffles.

Jenny giggled. A sound, not unlike tiny tinkling bells Ian once heard a long time ago in a church. Sweet and clear.

"They'll be early," Jenny said, completely unaware of his discomfort. "We're looking at maybe a month at most. Not too terrible a wait, Tuck. You'll be fine. Take up knitting or something."

Amelia shot her a glare with a faint growl. One he knew Jenny could not see, but the maid laughed. There was no doubt she knew her friend well.

"Twins, I canna believe it," Colin rasped.

"Two hellions to drive you sorely mad. Now that 'twill be a delight to see," Ian said.

"Would you care to hear their heartbeats?" Jenny asked Colin.

"Hear their..." he swallowed hard. "Aye."

He moved down the side of the bed while grasping Amelia's hand. Jenny handed him the stethoscope and he placed the tips in his ears. She felt her way down his arm and took hold of the disc and pressed it to Amelia's large belly. The smile and wonder that spread across Colin's face was a sight to see, one that warmed Ian deep inside.

With a tear glistening at the edge of his eye, Colin snatched the things from his ears and hastened to the head of the bed. He took Amelia's tear-stained face in his large hands and pressed a most gentle kiss to her lips.

Ne'er in his life had Ian e'er been jealous of his friend, not in truth, not until now. This overwhelming love before him was a wonder. It was a miracle, a gift, one he would never know, for he was not only a fourth son, but a bastard son.

His heart lay heavy on his chest as he watched his friends' loving display. He could not be happier for them, but it could not dissuade the emptiness surrounding his soul, for no woman of gentle breeding would ever want a bastard for a husband.

A sniffle to his right caught his ear. "Let us leave them to their privacy," Elspeth said with a faint clearing of the throat, and escorted Ian and Jenny from the room.

"Ian, you mind the lass while I tell Douglas of the news." Elspeth bustled off down the hall toward the Laird's chambers before he could protest.

"Would you care for a tour of the castle, Mistress Maxwell?" he asked awkwardly. "Or perhaps I can escort you to your chamber?"

"Um, a tour would be nice. Although I won't be able to see much of anything."

He let out a long harsh sigh, but decided to leave the old argument alone this time, and slipped her hand onto his arm. As they wandered the halls, little was said between them, other than Ian's comments about the rooms.

Upon entering the solar, he introduced her to Douglas, Colin's father and the Laird of the clan, who sat with a very large smile on his face beside Elspeth in front of the fireplace.

"Would ye believe I'm about tae become a grandfather? Of twins, no less?" the old man said with hearty laugh. "I thank ye for coming tae Amelia, lass."

"I'm glad to be here," Jenny said softly. She felt Ian's gaze with that statement. Slowly, she turned toward him. "Thank you for bringing me. I *am* glad I came. Even without my glasses."

Ian bowed and escorted her to a chair. "I will do my best to find what you need, mistress." He sat near her on a sturdy bench.

"What does the lass need?" Douglas asked.

"Her spectacles, dear," Elspeth said. "They were lost on her journey."

"Ah. Edinburgh. 'Tis the place to find such things. Or mayhap as far as London."

"Agreed. I shall leave at first light, and if not successful, I shall venture on until I am," Ian said.

Jenny shook her head at him. "You'd have to bring back dozens in hopes that one might assist me. No, the odds are slim to none at best that you would succeed. As I stated earlier," she said. Why couldn't he see that it was useless? It served no purpose other than to raise false hopes? Would it kill him to agree with her just once?

"I have faced worse odds, believe me," he said.

"I'm sure you have, but this is a fool's errand."

"I am determined in this, mistress," he said, his voice tight.

"You won't find any," she said through clenched teeth.

"I am sure that I will."

"And I am sure that you're a—"

"Children," Elspeth interrupted.

The Laird chuckled brightly. "This U—S breeds spirited lassies, eh Ellie?"

Elspeth laughed softly. "Aye, that it does, love."

Jenny ground her teeth, knowing full well she would regret it later. The headache and the damage to her teeth weren't worth it, but this pious man beside her brought out her temper with full force whenever he spoke. It was so unlike her. She normally avoided confrontation, loathed it, but ever since she'd met Tuck nothing was the same. She'd changed, but was it for the better?

"Why not take the lass with ye, Ian lad? My Ellie says Amelia isna due for a while. Seems there would be enough time fer ye tae fetch her the things and be back in time."

"'Tis not necessary. I assure you."

Jenny's head swam. Go on another adventure? Did she dare? Although it would be fruitless as far as finding any glasses, she could experience so much more of the era. Even blind it would be impossible to miss the sounds and smells of Edinburgh. "I think it's a wonderful idea," she said.

"'Tis a terrible idea," Ian said. "You will not go."

"Why not?"

"Because I said nay."

"That's not a reason."

"'Tis good enough for me."

"Well, it isn't good enough for me."

"Your opinion in this matter is of no import," he said with a low growl.

"My opinion is the only one that matters."

"The opinion of a mule-headed woman is worthless!"

"Mule-headed? You're the one who's mule-headed and my opinion is not worthless!"

"For the love of God!" Douglas blustered. "If 'tis what she needs tae aid in the birthing of my grandchildren then go she must!"

Jenny jumped at the Laird's command, but regained her composure quickly. "And go I shall."

"I can retrieve her spectacles more quickly if I go alone," Ian said, his voice strained.

Douglas sighed. "Aye, ye could travel faster alone, but ye need the lass tae do the choosin'."

"Exactly," Jenny said with a smirk in Ian's direction. "You need me." She could feel the heat of his temper wafting off him in low undulating waves.

"Wonderful! 'Tis settled then," Elspeth said.

"What's settled?" Tuck asked shuffling in with Colin by her side.

"You're supposed to be in bed," Jenny said.

"Waddling in here can't be bad."

"Doctor's orders. Get her in bed," Jenny ordered Colin.

Tuck swatted at her husband's hands. "In a minute. I still don't know what's settled."

"Ian and I are leaving for Edinburgh tomorrow to get me some new glasses."

Ian shot to his feet. "We most certainly are not!"

"Of course you are, dears," Elspeth said. "Oh, you'll have such fun, lass. 'Tis such a large city, oh the sights you'll see. Well, once you've found your spectacles."

Jenny and Elspeth chattered back and forth, ignoring Ian's constant attempts to interrupt.

A shrill whistle split the air and all eyes turned to Tuck now seated in a chair by the fire, her feet propped up on a stool. "How long does it take to get there?" she asked.

"'Tis three days at least." Three long days and nights, Ian thought. And all with this irritating woman constantly by his side. He would either kill her or, heaven help him, kiss her again.

"Do you think you'll be back in time before I drop my load?" Amelia asked.

Jenny shook her head. "Not if you don't stay in bed."

Amelia grumbled, something obscene, Ian was certain, but could not hear it clearly.

"Look, I'm ninety-eight point five percent sure I'll be back in time," Jenny said. "If you stay in bed. And after all, I'm not going to be much help if I can't see what I'm doing."

"True," Amelia replied with sigh.

"You cannot mean to say you agree with this?" Ian asked, praying Amelia would reconsider.

"You'll keep her safe," she said off hand.

"Can you ride, lass?" Colin asked.

"The woman is afraid of horses," Ian said, a bit more smugly than he'd intended, but it was a fact she could not deny, and 'twould surely win his argument.

"Oh, well, um, yes. I'm afraid that's true. Not as much as I was before," Jenny added quickly. "But I don't know how to ride."

"There then, you see? 'Tis lunacy for her to accompany me."

"You'll just have to lead her horse," Amelia said.

"It will likely take longer than three days at that pace, but, aye, it can be done," Colin said.

"But—but—"

"Is that still within my time frame, Jen?" Amelia asked, ignoring Ian's pathetically sputtered pleas.

"It merely lowers the percentage to approximately ninety-five point nine percent."

"This is insane," Ian muttered.

"Och, but the lass canna travel looking like that," Elspeth said.

"Good point. Your dress doesn't exactly fit," Amelia

said with a chuckle. "And your jeans will be too unusual."

"Aye, the fuss those blasted trews made when you wore them, love," Colin said with a wink to his bride.

"Why do I feel as if I am not in the bloody room?" Ian asked, but no one paid him any heed.

"Simple. Ye dress the lass as a boy," Douglas said. "She's but a wee thing and could pass as one without trouble."

"I'll not be cuttin' that child's hair tae stuff under a cap," Elspeth fussed.

Ian's gaze shot to the long braid hanging down Jenny's back. Nay, he would not let them do such a thing, not even the woman herself. Not until he had the chance to see the rich tresses unhindered and about her shoulders and hanging to her tiny waist.

He shook the notion from his head. What did he care what the woman did with her hair? The trip through time must have stolen his good sense. Aye, it had addled his wits for certain.

"Fiona and I can take in a few dresses," Elspeth said. "You'll simply have tae wait another day or two before you set off."

An odd weight lifted from Ian's chest. He suspected it had to do with them not cutting her hair, but refused to give it anymore thought. The entire thing was lunacy. "'Twould be much simpler if I went alone," he said. "And you have added more days onto this journey. I am sure we will not be back in time now," he reasoned aloud, praying it was true.

"Yes, it does lower the percentage a bit more, but it's still within the range of expectancy," Jenny said matter-of-factly.

He had to think fast. This would not do! Then it came to him. Resting his arm along the mantel he addressed the mad group. "You all seem to forget that there are no inns between here and Edinburgh. The lady is not accustomed to sleeping on the ground. And in such weather as this," he said, motioning toward the window and the falling rain.

"Hmm, true," Amelia said with a thoughtful nod. "You're a wimp on a trip, Jen. He's got a point there. Cold, hard, wet ground, no soft fluffy pillow, no room service.

It'll be tough. You sure you want to do this?"

"I happen to be a human being, not a porcelain doll," she said with a wry grin. "I'll survive, I assure you."

"Works for me, then," Amelia said.

"But she has no maid to accompany her!" Ian said, casting out his last and only hope. "Her reputation would be in ruins."

Amelia laughed, as did Jenny, bringing a deep scowl to Ian's brows along with a monumental headache.

"Oh, my yes," Elspeth said with a frown, lifting Ian's hopes, but only briefly.

"Not a problem," Amelia said. "Where we come from women travel without chaperones all the time. And that's the only place her rep matters."

"I'm no' so sure I care for that." Elspeth turned her hard gaze to Ian. "But I know you will be a gentleman at *all* times and protect her."

Ian could only nod, his voice lodged in his throat.

"Well then, in that case come lass, we'll go find you some things for the trip while Colin gets Amelia back tae her bed," Elspeth said.

Ian's arm fell to his side, his mouth agape. This couldn't be happening. He was doomed.

Jenny and Elspeth disappeared through the door, while Colin and Amelia shuffled across the room. Douglas sat smiling smugly, the old dog.

"You should take someone with you in case you run into trouble, though," Amelia said over her shoulder. "Jen won't be any help without her glasses, and she's not trained for combat."

"You could have fooled me," Ian muttered.

Amelia paused with a chuckle. "Oh, I so have to hear the whole story."

"Aye, love. I am curious myself," Colin added with a broad grin.

Ignoring them, Ian asked, "And whom do you propose I take on this ridiculous farce of a quest?"

"Michael would be my pick," Amelia said with a nod.

"Aye, he has exhausted the area for a gift for Fiona. Nothing seems tae suit the lad. I'll wager he would like tae see what Edinburgh has tae offer."

Ian cast his eyes heavenward. "This is utterly

insane." He was burdened with a lunatic scientist who could not see, was terrified of horses, and had no inkling of how to travel in his time, and a moony eyed lad searching for the perfect gift for his betrothed.

They had all lost their minds, and he was about to lose what was left of his.

Chapter Four

Jenny woke with a start, not sure where she was, then in a flash, it all came back and she smiled. It took only a moment for her smile to fall, however. Her feet and hands were like ice. The romance of the age was quickly lost. The only thing that would make her current condition worth suffering would be someone to warm them.

She sighed and chastised herself for her silly thoughts. She knew what had brought them on, or rather, whom. "I am such a pushover," she grumbled and snuggled down deeper beneath the covers. Ian's charm wasn't a complete loss on her, although he'd yet to direct any of it to her specifically. And if he ever did, she would be in big trouble.

There was a knock at the door.

"Who is it?"

The door opened and Jenny peeked out from the covers.

"Hey Jen, you okay?" Tuck asked as she waddled in. Someone followed her carrying a tray. "Over there will be great. Thanks, Fiona."

She placed the tray by the fireplace, then stoked the smoldering embers to a warming blaze. "Can I do anything else, Tuck?"

"No, that's great. Thanks." With that Fiona left.

"So, you gonna sleep all day or what?" Tuck asked.

"I'll crawl out when it's warm. How do you stand it?"

"I've got a natural bed warmer," she said with a chuckle.

Jenny didn't need to be reminded of that, especially when she was just thinking about one for herself. "Speaking of bed, you're supposed to be in it."

"Oh, come on, Jen. I can't stay in bed, I'll go nuts. You and I both know it. But I'll spend more time off my

43

feet, okay?"

"Please, Tuck, you've got to take this seriously. You may be as strong as an ox, but you still need to rest. A lot."

She sighed heavily. "Okay. I promise. I'll behave, right after we have a little visit before you take off. Now, come over here, you'll be warmer by the fire," she said as she angled herself into a chair.

Wrapping all the covers she could around her frozen limbs, Jenny joined Tuck by the fire. Something hot steamed from the bowl on the tray.

"Eat up, it'll help."

Jenny tentatively tasted the concoction and found it quite pleasant. As she ate and got warm, Tuck filled her in on things. They'd really not had a chance to just talk. Although for Jenny it had only been a day since they'd parted in the twenty-first century, for Tuck it had been almost a year.

"You know this is just a taste of what the road's going to be like. You sure you want to go with Ian?" Tuck asked.

"I don't really have a choice. He can't, regardless of what he says, find the glasses I need. And I'm not much use to you without them." She kept her suspicions of not finding any at all to herself. She didn't want to ruin Tuck's hopes.

"Okay, if you're sure. But honestly, you don't think you'll find any do you?" Tuck asked.

Jenny giggled. "You haven't changed, not really, not when it gets down to it. You can still read me and, I imagine, everyone else."

"Hey, just because I'm married and carrying this load with me, doesn't mean I'm getting slack." She snorted. "Heck, before I knew I was pregnant I was still tossing the guys in the lists. And I will again just as soon as these guys make their debut," she said, rubbing her belly.

"Colin doesn't mind that you still practice hand-to-hand combat?"

Tuck laughed. "Are you kidding? Who do you think gets put on his back the most? The man is damn stubborn, but he isn't stupid. He knows better than to try and change me."

Jenny sighed. "Which is why you love him so much."

"Oh, that and a few other reasons," she said with a chuckle that faded quickly. "You know, I have you to thank for all this. If you hadn't figured out how to get me back here, I'd probably be at the bottom of a bottle right now."

Jenny straightened, her smile gone. "No you wouldn't. You're stronger than that, Tuck. One binge when you thought Colin and all this was lost to you doesn't make you an alcoholic." A small smile tilted up her lips. "And after the hangover you had, I doubt you'd have ever so much as looked at another bottle again, much less drink from one."

They both chuckled. "You're right. But thanks, anyway."

"You're welcome."

"Oh, I almost forgot. Colin has a request. He wants to know if you can teach Maggie, she's the cook, how to make Gummy Bears."

"You got him hooked too, huh?" Jenny asked, and Tuck nodded. "Well, I won't promise that they'll be bear shaped, but I'm sure I can concoct something when I get back."

"Thanks. I know he'll appreciate it. And I wouldn't mind either. Pregnancy cravings when there's no all-night market around is hell."

"Oh, I bet it is. That and no pizza delivery, or ice cream, or chocolate."

"Stop, stop! I can't take it!"

The both laughed hard. It felt good. Really good, and was yet another reminder of how much Jenny was going to miss her best friend when she went home.

"So, once you're fed and warmed up, how about we take a tour?" Tuck suggested.

"You have no business wandering around the castle. Anyway, Ian took me on a tour last night," she said, and concentrated on her food or else the keen-eye of Amelia Tucker would know too much. If she didn't already.

"Really? Well, well, well."

"Stop it, Tuck. I know you said he was gorgeous, and nice, and charming, but honestly, he isn't about to be interested in me. So drop it right now. And in case you haven't noticed he can't stand the sight of me."

"Nope, I'd say you're wrong about that. I've seen how he looks at you, but you two do know how to go at it," she said with a snicker.

"Um, how does he look at me?"

"Ohhhh, like a man who's interested."

Jenny couldn't help the small snort of disbelief. "Oh sure. He's interested. He's interested in testing out the latest in sixteenth century torture techniques. Next thing you'll be telling me is that he actually likes me."

"There isn't a woman on this planet that man doesn't like."

Oh what a comfort that was. "Well, he isn't exactly falling at my feet, so we don't need to discuss him anymore."

"Okay," Tuck said, and sat very still and silent.

Jenny could feel her eyes boring into her. "Stop it. You're not going to convince me he's interested."

"I didn't say a thing."

"No, but you thought it."

Tuck huffed. "Well, why not? I know you like him. You can't lie to me. I've seen how you—squint at him. All that tall, blonde, broad-shouldered testosterone is hard to miss, even without your glasses."

"I'm not his type, and you know it."

"Oh, please. You're not exactly a dog, you know. I'll admit you're brain probably scares him witless, but the rest of your packaging is in good shape."

"Gee thanks."

"If it's not the fighting, and not the packaging, then what is it? Oh, wait. It's the time thing, right?"

"Something like that," Jenny lied.

"Okay, so you're just visiting, and well let's face it. The commute would be hell, but that doesn't mean you can't have some fun while you're here."

Fun, right. The thought of a fling was an intriguing idea, but it would never happen. Even if she threw herself at the man, he'd manage to tactfully decline. She just wasn't his type. She was surprised Tuck didn't realize that.

"Love and impending motherhood has obviously altered your thinking," Jenny said.

Tuck nodded. "Possibly, but I also know when I'm

right about something. You like Ian and Ian likes you. Of course I knew you'd like him. Remember I'm the one who told you about him. You should've seen your eyes light up. But I suppose the real man, and your lack of glasses, has tempered that a little. He isn't quite what you expected, is he?"

Jenny shook her head. "Not quite, no." So far he was irritating, stubborn, and could kiss like nobody's business. Not to mention she nearly melted at the mere sound of his voice.

She held in her sigh as she took another bite of her breakfast. She'd always known that someday her silly Cinderella dreams would turn on her. She'd found Prince Charming, well a different version, but she had no doubt he was all that Tuck claimed. Only problem was, Prince Charming wasn't interested.

"Look, I can see you're not too comfortable with this topic, so I'll drop it. For now," Tuck said. "Finish up your breakfast and we'll go down to the kitchen, my favorite spot these days," she said with a chuckle, "and meet the rest of the gang."

"You are going back to bed."

"Come on. I promise I'll behave the moment you and Ian take off."

"No, now."

The door opened with a bang, making Jenny jump. She almost wore what was left of her breakfast.

"There you are," Colin growled as he stomped over to Tuck. "You ne'er do as your told, woman."

"Don't start that woman crap with me MacLean."

"I'll start whatever I bleedin' like." He bent over and scooped Tuck up into his arms as if she didn't weigh a thing. Of course he was a massive piece of work himself.

"I can still walk, Sasquatch," Tuck mumbled, but linked her arms around his neck.

"Aye, that you can, mavourneen, and I can still carry you." Colin turned and gave Jenny a nod. "I'll do better, I promise you. She'll no' get out of bed again. If I have tae keep her there myself." He headed out the door, his burden not slowing his stride.

"Come see me when you're dressed, Jen," Tuck called out as they disappeared down the hall.

Jenny smiled as she felt her way across the room and closed the door. They were a pair. And Ian?

"A fling." She sighed heavily as she leaned back against the door. "Not going to happen. The odds are..." With a grimace, she quit calculating. They were pretty bad. Not surprising. She'd done it once before, but it hadn't meant to be a fling on her part.

Steven Collier, a med student in one of her many classes back in college, had been the one she thought she'd spend the rest of her life with. She'd assumed he was serious about her. After all, the man had waited months before making any real advances. So naturally, when he finally got her into bed, she thought he was the one.

She was wrong. But how could she have known that a couple dozen dates were nothing in the scheme of things to Steven? She had no idea the lothario was dating half the women in her graduating class.

There were others she considered dating after him, actually went out with a few colleagues once in a while, but never anything serious, and never ever more than an innocent goodnight kiss. She no longer trusted her ability to gather accurate information on the human male. It wasn't as if they were complicated, not in the least, but she could never determine if they were sincere. So for safety's sake, nothing serious, which calculated to no flings. Flings were serious.

She sighed with a shiver as she pulled on her dress. "At least they are to me." And therein lay the problem. No flings, meant no Ian. Even if he were open to such a suggestion, he would be too easy to fall in love with, and that complication she did not need.

A disgusted huff burst past her lips. He may be Prince Charming, but she was lousy Cinderella material. A pretty dress and a pair of glass slippers wouldn't make a difference where she was concerned.

****

Vernon wasn't afraid of hard work, but a peasant's life was definitely not for him. His stolen clothes scratched horribly and smelled. But it was his only choice if he wanted to gain entrance to the castle. He had to find Jenny Maxwell and get the hell out of there.

Toting a load of kindling, he followed one of the servants into the castle and to the kitchen. Somewhere along the way he'd break away and look for Maxwell's daughter.

"Maggie, we need tae ready enough food for Ian's journey," an old woman said as she bustled into the kitchen, her arms filled with dresses. "We've little time tae tarry about. Can you see tae it while Fiona and I work tae make the lass' gowns fit?"

The cook said something Vernon couldn't understand, but he didn't really care. The Englishman was leaving, which meant one less man guarding his quarry.

"Good. Come Fiona. We've little time tae get Jenny fitted well and proper," the old woman said, and motioned for one of the younger girls to follow. "We canna have the lass lookin' like a rag-a-muffin in Edinburgh."

Edinburgh? Interesting. The brat was going with the Englishman. Although he would have to deal with her new bodyguard, snatching Maxwell's daughter from the road would be a lot easier than getting her out of the castle. Still he carefully noted the stairs the women took. Knowing the layout of the castle might be to his advantage at a later date, but he couldn't get up those stairs now. There were too many people, and he couldn't chance getting caught.

He left the kitchens and headed for his hiding place in the wood, not far from the road. There he would wait.

****

Two days later, after hugs from Tuck, whom Jenny had ordered straight to bed—again—and a hug from Elspeth and Fiona, Jenny, Ian, and Michael were on their way.

They'd been riding for nearly an hour, when Jenny couldn't take the silence any longer. "You know you could've avoided all of this," she said to Ian's brooding back. And he was brooding. He'd avoided her the last two days. He'd even made himself scarce while Michael helped her get more accustomed to sitting on a horse and being led around. It wasn't easy to get over her fear of the animal, but the mount chosen for her seemed docile enough, and she was determined.

Ian hadn't spoken a word to her since they'd started out that morning, and Michael wasn't much for conversation. His favorite and only topic was Fiona. Jenny needed a good mental exercise to get her mind off of things, like glasses, horses, pregnant women, love, and Ian Southernland was just the man to do it. So to speak.

Shaking off the dangerous avenue of her thoughts, she focused on her goal. Conversation. "If you'd planned better—" she said, and as expected was promptly interrupted.

"I tried to persuade you not to come," he said, facing forward.

"I meant the first night we met."

He groaned at the age-old argument, bringing a crooked grin to her mouth.

He tossed the lead to Michael and let his horse fall back along side hers. "I was not willing to take that risk," he said.

"Through clear and deductive reasoning the conclusion is unavoidable. There was no risk."

"Deductive reasoning based on inaccurate information provides inaccurate results," he said.

"True. However, my information is not faulty and is based on sound experimentation." She almost smiled, enjoying this odd little banter. And this time he couldn't interrupt their debate by picking her up, she thought smugly.

"Incomplete experimentation. More, much more is required."

She knew she should be getting angry, as usual, but the steady gate of her horse lulled her into a more complacent mood. Maybe because she remembered Ian's vow not to let anything happen to her. Silly thought, really, but it helped. It helped quite a bit, knowing that he cared, in his own way. She now had two people who cared about her. On vastly different levels, yes, but still that was more than she had before coming to Scotland so many months ago.

"I will experiment more. When I return home," she said, forcing her thoughts back to their discussion.

"You mean that one more trip will prove your theories?" Ian laughed. "Not much of an experiment."

"It'll have to be enough. I can't risk causing any problems with a lot of *traveling.*" She knew they had to be careful how they discussed the portal. Although Michael was probably daydreaming about his fiancé, they didn't need him hearing them discuss something so unusual.

"Where is your sense of adventure?" Ian sighed. "The sites one could see, 'twould truly be amazing. The torch," he said dropping his voice low. "Automobiles, airplanes, and the other many wondrous things of your time. I would have enjoyed seeing them."

She turned her head and squinted, desperate to see if he was teasing or not. "Are you saying you wish you'd stayed? Are you actually admitting that I was right?"

He straightened in his saddle. "Nay, do not be ridiculous. I made a vow and was honor bound to keep it."

Jenny grinned. "But you're curious. You want to know what it's like, being there, I mean."

"Aye," he said, and she clearly heard a wistfulness in his voice and they both fell silent for a time.

He was everything she imagined her Prince Charming would be, well as far as she could tell. The way he sat on his horse, his sharp mind, the seductive tone of his voice, and how well the man kissed—his best feature by far.

She snorted softly. Like she was an expert, but she knew *wow* when she felt it. A simple word—wow—but she could think of no better way to describe it. But he was from the past, a time not her own. So what was the point in thinking about him?

A sigh slipped from her lips. No, time wasn't the problem. The problem, her keen logic pointed out, was that she wasn't the man's type. And this particular breed didn't settle for one woman. So what if he wanted to see her time, it wasn't likely to happen. Even if he did go back with her for a visit, he wouldn't stay with her. There were too many beautiful women in the twenty-first century, all very accessible and very eager to have a taste of a man like Ian Southernland.

Although she couldn't really see him, Tuck had been very thorough in her description of the rogue. She had a clear image in her mind of what he looked like aside from the charming smile, the wonderfully fit body, and those tempting blonde curls. All of which left her with no doubt that he would be extremely popular in her time as he was in this one. What woman didn't love a roguish prince?

He turned his head in her direction, and she quickly shifted her gaze to the road.

****

Ian studied her as they plodded along. The sunlight was kind to her in many ways, but the soft warm glow it cast upon her delicate features would forever stay in his mind. Untouchable, was what it said. Not meant for him.

Blast her to perdition! He did not want this woman. She was argumentative, stubborn, and lacked any sense of adventure. While he yearned to leap into the unknown and explore the world around him, she preferred to walk through life according to some mental list she'd devised. Rules and strictures at every turn. Why, she would dissect the very essence of pleasure if she had her way. Oh, aye, he knew many things about Jenny Maxwell. Amelia had been most thorough in providing him with the information they thought he would need to find her and how to persuade her to come with him.

He clearly heard Amelia's words echoing in his thoughts. "She'll hand you a bunch of junk about her father needing her, but don't let her con you," Amelia had said. "He's a jerk and a half. He doesn't give a rat's ass about anyone but himself and his wallet. But I'm sure if you tell her I need her, then she'll come. She's got nothing else, anyway. Just her work, which she probably ran right back to after I left."

Ian wondered how Jenny would truly have fared in her time without Amelia by her side. There was a strong bond there. He saw it in her eyes, heard it in her voice, she cared deeply for Amelia.

A quirky grin stole across the maid's lips. Some private joke? Thoughts of her friend perhaps, or a memory? The memory of a kiss?

Dolt! She could not, would not wish to share the slightest dalliance with him. They were far too different, and she was but a visitor in his world. Once she returned to her time, she would do as Amelia had predicted and resume her work. Hiding, she claimed.

He frowned with the uncomfortable thought.

Although Jenny was most irritating at times, had no sense of adventure whatsoever, he detested the notion of this rare beauty living out her days cloistered away in some laboratory with no friends or loved ones by her side. She did not live life, if Amelia's words were to be believed. She merely existed.

But it didn't matter what she did with her life upon her return, he argued with himself. All that mattered was her safety now, and his determination to keep away from the woman. She was a lady. Out of his reach. Although recognized by his father, he was a bastard with no prospects. A lady would never venture so low. Not even one from the future.

Chapter Five

Riding for an hour, talking little along the way, they stopped to rest for a few minutes before moving on to Tobor Morar, a port from where they would take a boat across to the mainland.

Ian bit the inside of his cheek, knowing full well he would have to help the woman down from her mount. She not only couldn't see, she had no real knowledge of what she was doing. A few hours on a horse being led around the bailey did not make her a rider. He could ask Michael to do it, he supposed, but refused to let his desires, however unbelievable, get the better of him.

"We shall rest for a few minutes," he announced, and slid from his horse.

Michael nodded and dismounted. The lad held Jenny's horse steady as Ian slid his hands around her waist. The simple style of her gown, now quite fetching with the alterations, distracted him a moment as he lowered her to the ground. Aye, she was a shapely woman for one so small.

Her hands rested on his forearms while his remained secure around her waist. "Thank you," she said, her voice a bit shaky.

He could only nod, his tongue too thick to speak. 'Twould take but the slightest dipping of his head to kiss her, he thought.

"If you've a need tae some privacy, Jenny, there be a bit of trees over there," Michael said, wrenching Ian from his frozen state.

"Oh, um, thanks. I think that might be a good idea." Her face flushed pink, and Ian was struck once again by her beauty.

How could a woman such as her be alone? And of all the women in the world why did he have to lust after one that was so wrong for him?

She walked slowly, picking her way carefully across the small bit of road to the trees. Once there, he called out to her not to go too far. She waved and slipped into the thicket.

"I'll be taking tae the other side of the road," Michael muttered. But Ian could not take his eyes from the spot where Jenny had disappeared.

Something nagged at him, but he could not place the feeling. He'd thought all morn that 'twas nothing but his misguided lust and admiration for her bravery. He knew, although she sat prettily in the saddle, a sweet grin on her face, that she was frightened. But that was not what niggled at the back of his mind. There was something different about her. Different since the night they'd met, but he couldn't fathom what it was.

Shaking his head, he tended to his own business then found a half rotted log to rest upon while waiting for her to re-appear. Whatever the change, 'twould come to him eventually. After all, he was stuck with the woman for the next sennight.

****

Jenny felt silly squatting in the woods, but knew there was little choice in the matter. Several times she looked over her shoulder trying to determine if she was concealed enough, and several times she ran into a blasted tree.

The last one was rather large, so she decided that if she wasn't concealed enough behind it then she'd just have to trust Michael and Ian not to watch.

She took care of business as quickly as possible, then slowly turned back the way she came, her hands out in front of her so as not to run into yet another branch or tree. But unfortunately, the blurry leaves all looked the same and she wasn't sure which way led back to the road.

Feeling like a helpless twit, she opened her mouth to call out to Ian, then paused. She really didn't need this embarrassment. Oh, he'd never say a word, and neither would Michael, but it was so humiliating.

Standing perfectly still, she strained to hear them, or perhaps the horses, but all she heard was the wind in the trees...and something else. She wasn't alone. There was someone or something there.

At first she thought it was just one of the men standing close by, but she quickly reasoned that they would've said something. Especially after she ran into that tree. Then there was the chance it was an animal of some kind, but logic dictated that it would've run off with her stomping around in the woods. That left one other possibility.

The problem was, however, did she risk pure embarrassment and call out to Ian for aid, or did she let whoever was nearby do whatever it was they intended to do while she sat and waited?

Stupid she was not.

Jenny let out a blood-curdling scream, sure to bring Ian and Michael to her aid with the utmost speed, and send whomever it was lurking nearby on their way.

Barely a second passed as branches, leaves and such were crushed beneath heavy feet pounding toward her, while the unknown part of the puzzle cursed, although nearly imperceptible, and went in the other direction. A small grin slipped over Jenny's lips as she waited to be rescued.

It was rather nice, actually. No one had ever rescued her before. Her one brush with danger last summer had lasted all of a few seconds. Tuck had fallen into the fountain and Jenny had clobbered the kidnapper with her purse filled with entirely too many coins, succeeding in incapacitating him.

A slight blush crept up her cheek at the memory. Tossing pennies into every fountain in Europe wasn't going to get her what she wanted, but she deduced that it couldn't hurt.

"Christ woman!" Ian grabbed her arms, startling her from her thoughts, and ran his hands over her in search of injuries.

She knew she wasn't supposed to enjoy that part of the rescue, or was she? Since this was her first, she couldn't be certain what the rules were.

"Are you all right?" he demanded as a puffing Michael appeared behind him.

"Yes, I—" Wait a moment. The unknown person, a man she determined by the depth of his voice, had cursed in English. She quickly calculated the odds of the existence of another Englishman on the Scottish isle. One lurking in the woods, no less, and didn't care for the astronomical figure.

"Michael, go back to the horses and guard them," Ian said. "Quickly, man!" He scooped Jenny up and strode through the bushes at a near jog.

"I can walk," Jenny sputtered, while her thoughts kept cycling through the probabilities.

"I should not have let you venture off alone," he snarled.

She noted the rapid pounding of his heart against her side, and realized he wasn't angry with her, but afraid for her. He really did care. "I'm fine."

"Then why did you scream?" He did not stop until they stood beside her horse.

"Well, I—" She took a deep breath. "I got turned around, I didn't know which way was back."

His broad shoulders sagged as he let out a long harsh breath. "You could have called out for aid. Not screamed down the treetops." He lifted her to her horse and plopped her down on the saddle.

"I know that," she snapped. "I was about to when I realized I wasn't alone."

He turned toward his horse and paused. "You what?"

"I wasn't alone."

He shook his head and mounted his horse. Michael did the same. "This is going to be a long journey," he mumbled, tossing Michael the reins to her horse.

"But—"

Ian galloped ahead several yards leaving her stewing.

"Not alone," he murmured. The woman could not see! She wouldn't know if a full garrison was standing among the trees.

But that scream. God, he prayed he would never hear the like of it again. Never in his life had his heart pounded so fiercely, not even in the heat of battle. For a small woman she had lungs like a bull.

He slowed his horse to a walk, allowing them to catch up with him, but he would not ride beside her. The woman was twisting him in more ways than he could fathom, inside and out. Screaming, arguing, theorizing...kissing. Heaven help him. He would not be a sane man by the end of this journey.

He cast a glance or two her way and noted her brow furrowed in concentration. Some new argument simmering in her brain, no doubt. But thankfully, the woman said naught until they rode into the small port.

"What is the ratio of Scots to English on the island?" she asked.

"Beg pardon, lass?" Michael asked.

Ian cast his eyes heavenward in thanks that her latest undertaking was in learning more about the island's inhabitants and not a new way to torture him with her theories. "There is no ratio," Ian said. "None worth counting, at any rate."

She cast him a puzzled look. "I see."

Ian noted her brow furrow deeper with the information, and hated how much he longed to know what was going on inside her pretty head. Irritating she may be, but she was exceedingly bright, most of the time.

He moved to help her from her horse. Michael could've aided her, and he'd decided as much after their previous stop, but he found the strangest desire to not let another man touch her.

Ian blinked away the thought and grasped her waist. "Stay with us at all times. Do not wander off."

"Don't be ridiculous. I can't see where to wander." She peered around him at the bustle of the many people coming and going. "I do find it fascinating, just the same."

"I shall see to getting us across the loch," Ian said, handing the woman over to Michael. "Do not let go of his arm," he said, leaning close to her ear. "You would be a fine prize to a less than honorable man."

She cast him a look, but he noted her faint shiver. "Are you trying to frighten me?"

"I am only departing the truth, mistress. I shall return in due time." He walked away, her sweet puzzled frown bringing a grin to his lips.

"Was that some sort of twisted compliment?" Jenny hadn't meant to ask the question aloud and hoped Michael hadn't heard, but his low chuckle proved otherwise.

"I doona think he meant tae compliment you, so

much as warn you. You are a woman, and without a mon tae guard you, you would no' be safe."

Her feminist side bristled at the comment, but he was right. Without her glasses and armed with no more than a few defensive moves Tuck had taught her, she wouldn't hold up too well against a full assault. Her size was a very big hindrance in that regard, and from what she could see, all the blurry people hurrying about were a good deal bigger than her. Well, it was a port full of fishing vessels and the like, and fisherman had to be strong to bring in their catch so it made sense.

"But surely no one would accost me in broad daylight," she said.

"'Tis a port, lass. Full of all sorts. Ye canna be tae careful."

"I suppose." She hadn't expected things to be this dangerous, if Michael and Ian were to be believed, but there was that man in the woods. Perhaps she should've stayed at the castle after all.

****

Vernon cursed thoroughly. She'd evaded him again. He should've taken his chance in the woods and grabbed her. But the Englishman and the Scot riding with her— and their swords—made him think twice, and those extra seconds had cost him the opportunity. He would've had to shoot them, most likely. Not that he wasn't prepared to do that, but he'd rather not kill anyone if he could help it. Except for that snake, Maxwell. There was a man he wouldn't mind blowing away.

No sense in thinking on it now, he'd missed the opportunity. He'd heard enough to know they were in search of some new glasses for the brat. That would be troublesome, because if she saw him, really saw him, she might recognize him and ruin everything. He had to get her before she found any glasses. And with the mass of confusion around the boat, he might just find a way.

****

Ian was gone only for a few minutes, but long enough for Michael to answer Jenny's many questions regarding the fishing and other interesting tidbits about the port. It was that or dwell on what they'd said about her safety. She hoped they would find her a pair of glasses. She'd feel better if she could see, and hated missing so much. But that was yet another silly wish, another coin into another fountain.

"I really should've had Lasik surgery," she grumbled. Although she was a doctor, knew the procedure to be safe, the thought of having a laser anywhere near her eyes made her nervous.

"Had what?" Michael asked.

"Uh, I, uh—"

Ian chuckled as he stepped up behind her. It wasn't often Jenny was without coherent words. "We have but an hour's wait," he said.

She jumped with a turn. "Oh, so soon? How nice," she said, obviously relieved he had interrupted their conversation.

He took her arm and guided her to the boat, while Michael followed with the horses. "I know I should not ask, but I cannot let it lie," he said, too curious for his own good. "What was it that had you stammering so? It is not like you to be without a prompt reply."

"Oh, you're too funny. As if you don't have an answer for everything. The wrong answer, but an answer nonetheless," she said with a grin.

He chuckled, enjoying her wit and the many envious stares cast his way, although he knew he should not. "Tell me. Please. Michael is tending our horses and will not hear."

She nodded then let him assist her onto the boat. "I was just complaining about something I should've done a long time ago."

"And that was?" He escorted her to a vacant spot along the rail.

"Well, if you must know, I was wishing I'd had Lasik Surgery."

"And what would this surgery accomplish?"

"It would permanently change the shape of my corneas. The clear covering of the front of the eyes."

"Amazing. And this would allow you to see without your spectacles, I assume."

"For the most part. I wouldn't have perfect vision, but I wouldn't be blind either."

"And why have you not had this surgery?"

She pulled her gaze from the water and looked at him, her head cocked saucily. "If someone said they were going to cut on your eye with a small dagger, would you let them?"

"Ah, well, when put in that way, I can see your unease. But is this not a well tested technique performed by skilled men?"

She smirked. "And women, yes." Her ire faded quickly. "But it's still scary, no matter how you look at it."

"Aye, 'tis a bit unsettling. When you return, are you going to have this procedure performed?"

She let out a long sigh and looked to the rolling surf. "Probably. If this trip has taught me anything, it's the value of seeing." A small laugh slipped from her lips with a shake of her head. "You know, I had an extra pair of glasses in my bag in the car. If only I'd carried it with me when Tuck and I snuck into the gardens at Raghnall Castle."

"You look back too much and too often, mistress. You must look around you at the world you are in, and not through a microscope."

Her gaze shot to his. "How do you know about microscopes?"

He grinned and leaned against the rail. "I have had many talks with Amelia over these last months. Her internment has forced her to find other ways of spending her time."

The soft sweet laugh he enjoyed bubbled from inside her. "I suspect Colin has been after her for some time to take it easy. No wonder my sending her to bed for the rest of her pregnancy ticked her off."

"Aye, he has done his best to keep her off her feet and resting as much as possible."

She nodded. "It's a good thing, she could've delivered too early and lost them."

"That, I fear, would kill Colin."

"It wouldn't do Tuck much good either."

They fell silent for a long time, thoughts of their friends on their minds.

The ferry began its journey toward the opposite shore, and Ian's contemplation was interrupted. His singular thought lay in putting the slight rocking of the ship from his mind. He did not care for the sea, but felt confident that he would make it across the loch before anything untoward could happen.

A bout of cursing and a splash drew their attention.

"What's going on?" she asked.

He chuckled at the man floundering in the surf. "'Twould seem there was a stowaway."

"Oh no! What if he can't swim? What if—"

Ian gripped her arm before she made some dashed stupid decision to jump overboard and save the sorry sod. "The man is fine. Aye, he is swimming to shore," he said, pointing toward the fellow.

"Oh, thank goodness," she murmured, squinting in that adorable way of hers and tried to see the man as he made his way to shallow waters, but he knew she could not see him.

"You realize, 'twould you who would be drowning if you had attempted to save him." He couldn't refrain from smiling. This woman, blind to her surroundings, was willing to jump in and try and save a complete stranger.

Her head turned from her study of the shore growing smaller in the distance. "I—" she let out an exasperated sigh. "You're right. I would've sunk to the bottom in this dress." She shook her head and looked to the loch.

"'Twas an honorable thought, but I, for one, am quite glad you decided against it."

She turned with a laugh. "Don't care for swimming, eh?"

He smiled back at her. "The loch is rather cold."

"Yes, it is," she said, her laugh fading. "It's approximately sixty-four degrees Fahrenheit this time of year. Although not freezing, hypothermia could still set in with long exposure. Water lowers the body temperature twenty-five times faster than air."

Ian's smile grew. Her mind never stopped, and he found that fascinating.

Michael appeared beside them. "Jenny, may I ask you something?"

"Of course," she said, and turned to the lad with one of her superior looks. One that said she could and would solve any problem he might present her. She was truly an amazing woman. He had known only one other with such confidence. Amelia Tucker MacLean. But hers lay in her physical abilities while Jenny's were mental. Both women were captivating.

And oft times most irritating, he thought with a small smile.

"While Fiona was helping you with your dresses and such did she no' say anything that might help me tae find the right gift for her?" Michael asked. "She willna tell me what she wants." The lad frowned with such intense vexation, Ian withheld the urge to laugh.

Finding the right gift for a woman was a difficult task, but all in sundry knew that Fiona wanted naught but a ring around her finger and for Michael to stop his dawdling and say the words that would bind them before a priest.

"Oh, well, no. I'm sorry, Michael, she didn't." Jenny fiddled with a bit of lace at her collar, her gaze settling on something in the distance. "Well, not exactly."

"I beg you tae tell me," Michael said painfully.

Her gaze came back to the lad's. "Well, she said she was nearly green with envy of Tuck. That she has the very thing she craves most."

"But what? What does Tuck have that she craves so?"

Ian chuckled and slapped a hand on the lad's back. "She wants to be a mother, you dolt! Marry the girl!"

Michael looked at Jenny. "Is that—do you think that 'tis what she wants? Truly?" he asked, his voice faint and high.

Jenny nibbled at her bottom lip with a contrite smile and nodded, fully distracting Ian from the conversation at hand. Her face, pinkened by the wind off the loch, her lips, now a deep red, teased him to distraction. And the taste of her, he well remembered the sweetness of her kiss.

"Why didna she tell me?" Michael scraped his fingers across his scalp as he stalked off muttering curses beneath his breath.

The lad's display stopped Ian from making a cake of himself. It would not do to kiss the woman again, in public, and when he'd not been asked. She would likely slap his face, and he would surely deserve it. She was a lady, after all. But the memory of her taste lingered on his

63

lips, and under the circumstances 'twas not good, not good at all, for the taste of anything reminded him of his stomach.

"I hope I did the right thing," Jenny whispered.

Ian did his best not to think on the rocking boat and focused his attentions on their conversation. "He shall be fine. We have all tried many times to convince the boy to get on with things, but he has a rather hard head."

"There seem to be a lot of those around here."

"Are you referring to me, mistress?"

"If the *hat* fits." She laughed and propped her hand at her waist, a movement he knew did not bode well for him. "At first I thought we'd just gotten off on the wrong foot, but you have proven, time and again, to be the most stubborn man I've ever met."

"I am not stubborn. You simply cannot abide for someone else to be right."

She opened her mouth, but not a word came forth. With a huff, she spun around and planted her hands on the railing. The argument, a more ludicrous one if there ever was, was not over. Nor was the roiling in his stomach.

With a whirl, she turned and poked him in the chest. "You are not only wrong, you're insufferable, arrogant, officious, and—and—wrong," she said with a firm nod.

He closed his eyes on a moan, fatigued by their argument and the incessant pitch and sway of the boat. "Another time, mistress, and I would argue with you— gladly—but alas I cannot at present." He turned and made his way to the opposite railing where he was sure to lose his morning meal.

Jenny watched Ian's awkward gait as he crossed to the other side of the boat. What was the matter with the man? Then she witnessed his problem as he leaned over the railing. He wasn't one for sailing. She, on the other hand, was fine as long as she could see land.

"Michael," she called, and the grumbling young Scot came up beside her. "I need some fresh water, would you get some for me?"

"Aye." He retrieved one of their flasks, and using a handkerchief she'd tucked in her pocket, Jenny doused it with water.

She thanked Michael then made her way to Ian's side. Somehow she'd managed to cross the small boat without bumping into anyone or anything. A small feat in itself.

Without a word, she pressed the cloth to his forehead. There was no ignoring how sick he was, since all he could do was moan. He didn't refuse her attention, not even a whisper of an argument, just a pathetically muttered thank you.

Strange, she hadn't taken care of anyone before, not like this. Although she held a degree, many degrees in various scientific and medical fields, she wasn't really a doctor. She didn't know how to take care of people. Oh, she could set broken bones, suture wounds and such, but it wasn't the same thing.

Ian took the flask and rinsed his mouth before sliding slowly to the rough planks beneath their feet. He propped his back against the railing, his long legs stretching out before him. Jenny settled beside him and continued to wipe his brow and worked her way down across his cheeks to his throat, praying she wouldn't poke her finger in his eye.

"You should not sit here with me like this," he muttered.

"Why not? Isn't it seemly?" she asked with a small laugh. He was sick, he needed attention, and present day convention wasn't about to stop her from giving it to him.

Although Tuck had explained that she didn't need an escort, Elspeth still gave Jenny an earful over the last two days about traveling with two single men and no one else.

Ian offered a harsh chuckle. "Nay, and you well know it. 'Tis bad enough you travel without a female companion, but to tend me this way suggests—"

"Oh, hush. I don't think anyone cares."

He straightened somewhat. "They do care, make no mistake. But perhaps your attentions are for the best. If you appear to be mine, 'twould save me a good deal of trouble."

"I don't think any sort of subterfuge is necessary," she argued, although the word *mine* fixed itself firmly in her brain. She hoped she could keep the thought from spreading.

65

"I think 'tis very necessary," he said, easing closer. "'Twould likely save me from having to kill that pair staring so intently at you."

"You can't be serious," she said, a false light tone to her voice. It wouldn't do her any good to look, she wouldn't know whom he was talking about, but the very clear memory of someone in the woods with her that morning came to the forefront of her mind.

"I am most serious," he said, his voice a deadly calm.

She glanced over her shoulder and looked around at the other passengers. No one seemed out of place, and none seemed to be watching her, but she really couldn't tell.

She dabbed at his upper lip and heard him swallow. "Do you need me to help you up to the railing?"

"Nay, there 'tis naught left," he said with a pitiful groan.

"It'll be over soon."

"Alas not soon enough."

She glanced once again around her at the many people then turned back to Ian. "I really wasn't alone this morning in the woods, you know," she whispered. "I know I can't see worth a darn, but there was someone there."

"An animal of some sort," he murmured.

She dampened her handkerchief again and pressed the cloth to his forehead. Her fingers touched on his curls, distracting her for a moment. She lifted a few strands from his brow then slid her fingers deeper into the mass as she bathed his brow. A man's hair shouldn't be this soft, she thought.

He moaned low, adding to the warm glow building inside her, but she forced herself back to what she had to tell him. She laid her handkerchief aside and returned her fingers to his hair. He didn't seem to mind.

"It wasn't an animal. I would've frightened it off," she said, sinfully enjoying herself.

"You screamed, quite loudly," he said with a rough chuckle.

"That was after I realized it wasn't an animal. After I screamed, I heard you and Michael coming and the man cursed."

He clasped her wrist and brought her hand to rest

against his chest. "You heard someone other than I curse?"

"Yes. He was approximately ten feet away, parallel from the direction you were coming." She tried to put the feel of his broad chest beneath her fingertips from her mind, but it wasn't easy, they still tingled from his soft curls. "I didn't see him, of course, but I distinctly heard him swear. And in English. Thus my query as to the ratio of Englishmen to Scots on the island."

"Michael!" Ian called and jumped to his feet, pulling Jenny with him. His arm wrapped around her waist and pressed her to his side. He wavered only slightly.

Michael appeared in mere seconds. "Aye?"

"Mistress Maxwell is quite certain there was someone in the wood with her this morn," he said lowly.

"Ah, so that be what the hollerin' were about," Michael said.

"We need to keep a sharp eye," Ian said. "We do not know who or why he was there, but I suspect it has something to do with our charge here."

"That isn't logical," Jenny said. "No one in this—here would be looking for me."

Ian cupped her cheek. "Perhaps not for the reasons you think, but I will not allow him the opportunity to achieve his goal."

"Nor I," Michael added. "The two behind my right shoulder have a keen interest in the lass, but I'd hoped was just a wee bit of envy."

"I noticed the same," Ian said, his grip on her waist tightening.

Jenny rubbed her brow with her growing headache. This trip was getting more and more complicated. As if waltzing through time without her glasses wasn't bad enough, she supposedly had some lunatic chasing her. Oh, and let's not forget her attraction to a rogue who slid effortlessly into every fantasy she ever had. If she did find any glasses worth wearing, she had the distinct feeling when she saw Ian Southernland for real for the first time she was going to be in very big trouble.

Chapter Six

Michael pointed toward shore. "We're coming in tae dock."

"You tend the horses while I escort the lady to shore," Ian said. He looked down and noticed Jenny rubbing her brow, her eyes clamped closed. "Are you ill?"

She sighed and straightened. "Just a headache. I'll be okay once we get on the road."

He grinned at her determined nature. Odd that she wasn't afraid like any other sensible woman. But then Jenny Maxwell was not like any woman he had ever known.

They made their way ashore and he paused before lifting her to her mount. It would be best if they could put some distance between the men from the boat and themselves. He gave a nod to Michael who seemed to grasp his intent.

Ian mounted his horse as Michael stole up behind Jenny. The lad then snatched her by the waist and planted her firmly behind him.

"What—"

"Hold on," Ian said, as he grabbed her hands and wound them around his waist.

Within seconds they were galloping out of the small town with Michael just behind leading her horse. Ian had not counted on the woman gripping him so tightly, nearly cutting off his breath, but he suspected she was terrified with the harried ride and he would not ask her to loosen her hold.

Miles away, they slowed to a steady lope then to a walk. Jenny had yet to loosen her grip. He twisted in the saddle and pulled her around to sit across his lap.

"'Tis over, I promise," he said softly, her head pressed beneath his chin, her fists clutching his doublet.

"Are y-you s-s-sure?"

He rubbed her quivering limbs. "Aye, little one. Very sure." He cursed himself for terrifying her so, but they'd had little choice. Her rare beauty was attracting too much attention. The more distance he could place between them and others the better. He could deal with anyone who sought to harm or abduct her on the road more efficiently than when surrounded by a league of unknowns.

She lifted her head and peered about. "How long can I—I mean, how long do I have to ride like this?"

He bit back a chuckle. She was far too afraid to ride alone, even at a slow walk, but she refused to admit it. His horse was strong, however, and could carry them both for a while.

"I think we should ride double for a few more miles. Does that not suit you?"

"No, that's fine. Fine," she said with a small sigh and relaxed in his arms. The more he held her the more he felt she belonged there, but he knew that was not the case. Their differences were too vast, their lives too dissimilar, and he was not looking for a wife.

Liar, a voice whispered in the back of his mind. *Do you not recall your jealousy of Colin's life but a few days ago?* He clenched his teeth at the memory, but allowed the truth to settle over his brain.

Aye, he craved what his friend had, and could almost believe it possible someday, but this woman was not the one. He may lust after her, feel an overwhelming need to protect her, but he did not love her. Not as Colin loved Amelia. No, what Ian needed was a woman he had similarities with, a woman who shared his view of the world, one who had a thirst for adventure, and would keep him from ever wanting to wander. For if he ever did marry, he would be faithful. He would not be his father.

Ian vowed to prove the harpies of his youth wrong. He may look like Wallace Southernland, he may have his blood running through his veins, but he was his own man. But where does a bastard such as himself find a woman who could look on him in such a way?

"Can we stop for a minute?" Jenny asked, lifting the melancholy easing over him as she peered at him with those enchanting eyes of hers. "My leg's falling asleep."

"Aye. And I think 'tis safe enough for you to return to

your horse." Better there than in his lap where his body bade his mind to follow down a path he could not go.

The way she'd tended him as he fought against seasickness, the feel of her small hands in his hair, her warm body pressed to his. No, all would be better served if he kept a much greater distance between them. He was a man, after all, and could only resist so much temptation. For he suspected she was a woman who would keep him well and content in his bed.

They rode until the sun lay low in the sky before stopping for the night. Unfortunately, the weather had turned wet, but thanks to Amelia's incessant harping about Jenny not being accustomed to such travel, Ian had packed a large piece of cloth to suspend between a few trees for her privacy.

Yet with the weather as it was, he decided 'twould better serve if he hung the thing so they all could sleep in relatively dry conditions. The only problem, he feared, were the close quarters. Temptation lay nestled between him and Michael, her breast rising and falling with each soft breath. Amazed, he was that she had succumbed so quickly to sleep.

"Do you truly think someone is after the lass?" Michael asked quietly.

"I know not, but I shall not take nary a chance. Once we reach Edinburgh and an inn, we shall take turns standing guard outside her door during the night. Until then, we cannot let her out of our sight for one moment."

Michael chuckled. "She willna like that, I'll wager. She's a bit like Tuck with her independence."

"Aye, that she is. But she will have no say in the matter."

"Do you no' think those two men were eyein' her over much? Odd, I thought."

"Why odd? She is a beautiful woman."

"Och, no' nearly as pretty as my Fiona. But aye, she would be a prize tae some men. And most in the village know you've no wife and that I'm tae marry Fiona. She looks tae the world free fer the takin'. Still, she's so small and frail, and canna see. A mon wants a woman who willna break so easily. One that can work alongside him and give him strong bairns."

Ian cast a glance to the woman lying peacefully between them. "That frail woman held on with a firm grip during our dash from port. And I would not account it all to her fear of riding. No, she is not weak, my young friend. She has the sort of strength you cannot see, the sort many men would envy. And with her fey-like beauty she would be a prize on the arm of any man."

"I think you've gone daft on the lass," Michael said with a low chuckle. "But I've no' of a mind tae bandy that about," he added quickly. "I'd like tae keep my head. 'Tis your business and hers what goes on betwixt you."

Ian shook his head with a wry grin. Even love struck Michael could see his desire for Jenny. How many others saw the same? Colin knew of his attraction for her, but what of Amelia, and Lord save him, Elspeth, that matchmaking woman? And what of Jenny herself?

He glanced at her sleeping form, the subtle curve of her hip, the gentle rise of her breasts, that seductive bow-like mouth, begging to be kissed. It was a good thing she had no spectacles at present. She would see quite clearly every thought now speeding through his mind, and she would not be happy about it.

Trying to push his libidinous thoughts from his mind, he lay alongside her, his brow creased. What the devil was he going to do when she could see?

Duck, he thought, with a small chuckle.

****

The next day after a quick breakfast and a few hours of riding, they ate in the saddle. Not a pleasant way to spend one's lunch, but Jenny understood Ian's worry over their safety. A puzzle she had yet to decipher. Why would anyone in this time want to grab her?

Ian motioned for her and Michael to stay back as they came upon a farmhouse. A man came out of the barn just as Ian approached. Jenny couldn't hear what they were saying, but it looked congenial enough. The man wasn't pointing his rake or whatever it was at Ian in a rude manner. As a matter of fact they seemed well acquainted.

After a few moments, Ian motioned for them to come forward. "Donald here has given us permission to use his barn for the night."

Sleep in a barn. Oh joy. Well, barn or not, they'd be dry and would have more room to spread out. With a sigh she allowed Michael to lead her inside while Ian made some other arrangements.

At the moment, she could care less what they were she was so tired. Her knee hit a hay bale and she happily sank to the scratchy seat. Rubbing her lower back, she stretched and did her best to work out the kinks. What she wouldn't give for a hot bath and some clean clothes, and...food. Her nose twitched with the scent of something not the result of the many animals sharing her temporary hotel, and it smelled delicious.

"Innes, here, has some victuals for ye," the farmer said.

Through tired uncooperative eyes, Jenny spied a woman with a tray. With a sickening giggle, the girl handed Michael and Ian bowls of some sort. When it was Jenny's turn, she got a quick shove of whatever it was into her hands. The girl didn't stand there long enough to even see if Jenny had a good hold on it before rushing back to Ian's side.

Jenny chewed the inside of her cheek as she watched the girl hang all over him. She supposed the girl gave Michael a good deal of attention too, but Ian was her primary target. They were one big blurry blob. What bugged Jenny most was she couldn't tell if the girl was pretty or not. Only that she seemed to be tall, a bit on the buxom side, and long limbed.

Without tasting the fare, Jenny shoved spoonful after spoonful into her mouth. She didn't want to know what she was eating, and she didn't really care if it tasted good, her mind was otherwise occupied, as was her fuzzy vision. At least she resisted the urge to squint. It wouldn't help anyway, Ian and the girl were several feet away. No amount of squinting would bring any clarity to the picture before her, but she was well equipped with an imagination and knew that Ian was smiling and winking at the girl. All that nauseating giggling was proof enough.

Finally done with her meal, Jenny rose, crossed to the pair and shoved her empty bowl into the girl's hands. "Thanks."

With that she returned to her bale of hay, propped

her back against the wall, and wrapped the tartan Tuck had given her tightly around her, shutting them and everything else out. If Ian wanted to make an ass of himself, fine. It was none of her business how he handled his love life. But for some dreadful reason it hurt.

Ian watched as Jenny nodded off to sleep mere moments after she'd sat down. How she managed it was a mystery.

Once again, he tried his best to disentangle Innes from his arm. "Thank you, my dear. That was a fine stew." The last thing he wanted or needed was a scorned woman chasing after him. And truth to tell, as pretty as the girl was, he wasn't the least bit interested. Not this time.

"Is there no' else ye need?" she asked, her eyes filled with promises.

He cleared his throat. "Nay, but I, and my companions, greatly appreciate your hospitality. As always."

"Doona ye want tae go outside. Behind the barn? I have something verra interestin' tae show ye," she whispered.

He caught sight of Michael's broad grin before he turned his head. The lad would pay in the lists when they returned to Arreyder.

"My thanks, Innes, but I cannot—I cannot break my vows," Ian quickly lied.

"Och, ye canna mean it! Doona say ye married that one," she said in harsh whisper. "I ne'er thought ye'd e'er settle fer one woman."

That stung, as it was far too close to the very thing he did not wish to be—his father. But he only kept company with one woman at a time, and only a certain type of woman, at that. The kind sitting beside him. Not the sort he truly wanted.

His gaze strayed to the sprite seated across from him sound asleep. "Aye, I am quite leg shackled," he said softly, hoping not to disturb Jenny. And it wouldn't do for her to jump up and declare him a liar.

Michael, although still grinning, nodded in agreement. "Aye, well and done."

"Och, ye poor thing," Innes said with a tsk and patted

his knee. "A braugh mon like yerself shouldna' be burdened with a puny thing such as her. 'Tis a pitiful waste." She sighed and rose, still tsking and shaking her head as she left.

Ian turned to Michael who sat ready to burst with laughter. "'Tis not humorous."

"Nay, of course no'" the lad said, failing to hide his mirth.

Ignoring him, Ian shot to his feet and made a pallet nearby, then gently lifted Jenny and placed her on the makeshift bed. She made not a sound as he covered her with a blanket. How could anyone call her puny? She was slight of frame but well proportioned and strong of spirit. And a lovelier creature he'd be hard pressed to find.

****

A warmth at her back made Jenny want to snuggle in deeper, but the strong scent of hay filled her nostrils and reminded her of where she was. The question, however, was who or what was at her back.

An arm fell over her waist as a warm breath teased her neck. Okay, a man was at her back, and she knew full well it was Ian. She was grateful that it wasn't some barn animal, of course, but why did the man have to torture her this way? In all likelihood, he was completely unaware of her overwhelming attraction to him. The logical conclusion was that he'd grown cold and she was handy. He wasn't about to wrap his arms around Michael for warmth. But why not snuggle with his girlfriend?

Deciding that none of it mattered, not at the moment, she rose from her bed, one she didn't recall getting into, and left him to his dreaming. She didn't want to think of all the things he might have done or still wanted to do with Innes. Sensing a previous relationship between them had been as far as she let her mind wander. Further than that, her imagination would create some very vivid pictures in her head, although the main players would still be fuzzy since she'd not actually seen either of them.

"And I don't care to," she grumbled, knowing it for the lie that it was. She wanted to see Ian in the worst way. Aching to know if he was as handsome as Tuck described, as she imagined him to be with nothing but her blurry vision as a guide.

How many times had she looked at him and drawn in the details of his face with her mind's eye? Like a child's coloring book, she'd taken his outline and filled in everything. A smile that would make his eyes twinkle, lips just full enough to bring all sorts of decadent ideas to her head, and oh so much more. What if they did find her a pair of glasses and he wasn't as wonderful as she dreamed?

She'd be better off, she thought with a nod, and made her way outside.

Michael, already up and sitting outside the barn eating breakfast, told her where the privy was. She made her way across the barnyard and stumbled inside the boxlike structure. After dealing with the uncomfortable accommodations as best she could, she figured she was lucky she couldn't see well. The image of every nasty microbial she'd ever studied flashed through her thoughts.

Her task accomplished, she hurried out of the privy and started back across the yard as a figure burst from the barn in a bit of a panic.

Ian. She'd recognize that golden head anywhere, but what was he harassing Michael about? Did he usurp Ian's place with the farm girl last night? No, Michael wouldn't do that. He was too deeply in love with Fiona. Then what had her reluctant escort so upset?

Grabbing Michael by the shirt, Ian hauled the worthless lad to his feet. "Where the devil has she gone?" he demanded. "I told you she could ne'er be out of sight!"

The young fool swallowed his food and grinned stupidly. "I do love tae be right," he said.

He shook the insolent youth. "Where is she, man?"

With a chuckle, he pointed across the barnyard to where Jenny was carefully making her way in their direction. While her eyes squinted toward the ground beneath her feet, she kept one hand on the fencing at the edge of the yard, and the other holding her skirts up entirely too high, gifting him with a view of her lily white legs, sleek and slender.

Ian forced down the surge of lust as he shoved Michael aside then dashed off toward her. The terror pounding in his heart and in his head when he awoke to find her gone would be a memory he would not easily forget. He tried valiantly to attribute it to nothing more than a fear that he'd failed in his duty to protect his charge, but something deep inside said otherwise.

"Are you all right?" he said, grasping her arms and startling her.

"What? Of course I'm all right," she snapped, swatting at his hands.

"You are not to go anywhere alone," he seethed.

She shot him a cool, hard glare. "I had to *go*. Michael could see me the whole time," she said, squinting toward the barn. "I think," she muttered.

"I am responsible for you, woman, and would greatly appreciate better care on your part. When I say you are not to be alone, I mean you are not to be alone!" Twice she'd terrified him and he did not care for the feeling in the least.

"I'm not about to have you or Michael hold my hand while I'm—I'm indisposed!"

"Someone should have been standing guard by the bloody door!"

She rolled her eyes heavenward with a huff and resumed her precarious trek through the mud.

Time being of some importance, Ian plucked her from the muck and strode off toward the barn.

"I really wish you'd quit doing that," she growled. "I have two perfectly good legs."

"But not two perfectly good eyes."

She stiffened, and he regretted his words. She had two beautiful eyes, eyes he enjoyed looking into, although he shouldn't.

Michael came out of the barn with their horses saddled and ready to go. As Ian approached her mount, he tried to find a way to apologize, but for once in his life words failed him.

He placed her atop her horse but did not move away. There had to be something he could say to make amends. "I did not mean to offend you, little one," he said lowly.

"It was the truth." She turned to him, but her gaze refused to light on his face.

"In that they do not function well, aye. But that is all." He rested his hand atop hers on the pommel. "I rather like your eyes."

She stopped a tremulous smile. "They're just plain brown eyes. Nothing special."

Ian smiled. Even this woman, learned, stubborn, and constantly at odds with him, needed to hear a compliment, as women often do. "They are not plain, but quite extraordinary. As is the woman they belong to," he said truthfully.

She looked at him then, her smile a bit wider, then it quickly fell as her gaze lit on something over his shoulder. He turned, a moment of alarm that some criminal lurked there beat through his chest then settled to a normal rhythm as his eyes lit on Innes coming toward them. Ian smiled, although it was not a true one, and greeted the girl.

"I brought ye a few biscuits fer yer trip. 'Twill keep ye from hunger 'till ye next stop."

"I thank you," he said with a small bow.

She winked and went back to the house, a more happy sight Ian was hard pressed to see. He felt a bit like a rabbit having escaped the snare. Silly really, when he'd dallied with her and other maids of her ilk before. But this time the slightest hint of spending time with the girl didn't feel right.

"I'd like to get going, if you don't mind," Jenny said snippily.

Michael covered his chuckle with a cough.

Ian handed her the small bundle of biscuits then mounted his horse. They soon left the farm behind, but not Michael's grin.

Ian pulled his horse along side his. "Whatever you find so amusing, had best be well worth the cost, because once we return home, you and I shall have a go in the lists," he said low and firm.

Michael chuckled. "You canna see what's before your eyes?"

He sighed, hating the fact that he couldn't let that remark go. "Pray, enlighten me."

The young man looked over his shoulder at Jenny where she sat nibbling at a biscuit. "The lass is jealous, you daft mon. 'Tis plain as daylight."

"Ridiculous. She is not used to this form of travel and

has grown irritable with the ride. And what could she possibly be jealous of?"

Michael shook his head with a chuckle. "She may no' be able tae see Innes clearly, but a blind mon wouldna' have missed the history betwixt you."

"Nay, 'tis utter nonsense," he muttered. Even if the woman was of a mind, she was a lady. One entrusted to his care, not to his bed.

"Innes has a point, though," Michael said. "'Twill be difficult convincing others, those you know, that you married the lass."

"Innes did not appear too shocked," he muttered, not believing a word out of his own mouth. She'd been very shocked. She may even have suspected it was a lie, her wink at their parting making him pause. "We will continue the farce. 'Tis for her safety and reputation."

Michael eyed him. "If you were tae marry, 'tis Mistress Maxwell the sort of lass you'd choose?"

Ian looked back at the lady riding silently behind them. If he had a choice of all the women he currently knew and had ever known would she be among them?

He looked forward at the road, his jaw growing tired with his incessant clenching. "She is lovely, strong, intelligent, and determined, but nay. She and I would not suit," he admitted, hating the taste of truth on his tongue. Her stubborn nature, her need to live an orderly settled life, per Amelia's descriptions, was not for him, was not the sort of woman he could come to love. And, although he hated to admit it, he wasn't good enough for her.

Michael handed Ian the lead rein. "Then I suggest, Master Southernland that you leave the lass well alone, for she isna of the same mind." He fell back beside Jenny and chatted about Fiona and some of the sights they'd see in Edinburgh and the type of gift he should search for.

The lad was right about him leaving her well alone, but did he truly mean that she had feelings for him? Ian couldn't believe such a thing. Her jealousy, if it was truly that, did not necessarily mean she cared for him.

Still it made him wonder.

Chapter Seven

The day dragged on and Ian and Jenny barely spoke a word to one another. She was furious with herself for letting him make her feel this way. If he just hadn't complimented her, then she would've been able to forget all about him.

Do you enjoy lying to yourself, Jen?

"Oh shut-up," she mumbled.

"What's that, lass?" Michael asked.

"Nothing. I was just thinking out loud."

He chuckled and rode up beside Ian. She had the distinct impression that he was laughing at her, but wasn't sure what could possibly be so funny. They're trip had been anything but humorous. And it was all Ian Southernland's fault...and that farm girl.

"Stop it," she huffed softly.

"I'm thinkin' we need tae stop for a wee rest," Michael told Ian with a nod in her direction.

Ian looked back at her, and she could only assume, with a fierce frown. He sighed heavily and halted their little parade. It was just as well, her rear-end was numb and her stomach was grumbling.

Ian appeared beside her, his arms lifted to help her down.

"I can get down on my own, thank you," she said, and prayed her horse wouldn't move while she attempted it.

"As you wish," he said and stepped back.

With very little grace and no skill, Jenny grasped the pommel with both hands, lifted her leg over the saddle, and slowly lowered her foot to the ground before removing the other one from the stirrup. Only problem was there was no ground! And her skirts were riding higher and higher as she frantically wiggled her foot in search of it. Then her horse decided he'd had enough of her gymnastics and danced sideways.

Clutching the saddle as tightly as she could, she was about to let out a screech, when firm strong arms slid beneath her legs and around her back. She was once again in the single place she most wanted to be and should not be—in Ian Southernland's arms.

"Stubborn woman," he muttered.

She shot him her hottest glare as a few choice words developed on her tongue.

"Brave, but stubborn," he said, and strolled toward the trees with her still in his arms, her few choice words forgotten.

Another compliment. And yes, she thought with a sigh, she was stubborn. A streak she hadn't known she had until meeting this man. She surmised it was one of the reasons she was so well suited to research. The determination to not give up after a failed experiment, to forge on until all possibilities had been thoroughly tested. She'd just never realized how it might cause her to be less than congenial with people—with Ian. Perhaps it had more to do with her attraction to the man than her true nature.

"Sit here and rest while I retrieve our midday meal," he said, placing her on a log. When she didn't answer, he paused before turning away. "Do you need to find some privacy?"

She shook her head, studying him with her imprecise vision. He nodded then strolled toward his horse, but she could feel his gaze on her. Watching her. For her safety, of course, but there was something else, something new, and she wasn't exactly sure she wanted to know what it was.

"Oh, please. I'm making it into something else," she said to herself. She knew full well that she was doing anything and everything she could to make herself into Cinderella. Wanting him to notice her, pay attention to her, because of her and not some unknown threat she was no longer convinced existed.

Whoever had been in the woods with her hadn't done anything, and she had no proof that he would have. Perhaps she'd startled him as much as he did her. She may never know. But he was the reason Ian was watching her so closely, taking such pains to make sure she was safe. And he'd promised that he wouldn't let anything happen to her. No, if there was any attraction on his part, it was all in her mind. It was enough to make anyone irritable.

Michael and Ian sat beside her and they ate their lunch.

"We will be in Edinburgh tomorrow," Ian said.

"I thought it would be another two days, since you have to lead my horse."

He shook his head, the golden locks catching the few rays of sunlight piercing the cloudy sky. "Nay, our swift leave taking of the port made up for much of the time, as our taking the midday meal on horseback. 'Twill be late in the day when we arrive at the inn, however."

"An inn, with a real bed," Jenny said with a sigh that brought a few chuckles from her escorts.

They quickly finished their meal and returned to their horses. Ian lifted her up into the saddle, and she did all she could to put the feel of his arms from her mind. This was a necessity for him, not a pleasure.

"I really wish I could do this myself," she mumbled.

"You are too small, I fear," Ian said.

"If I had a shorter horse, I wouldn't be."

With a hearty laugh, he said, "Much smaller, little one, and you would be astride a pony."

The day waned and they finally found a small clearing off the road to bed down for the night. The sky was clear, and according to Michael filled with stars. Which meant it would be much colder than before. Jenny was grateful for being dry, but not too happy with the temperature drop. Especially since her libido kept explaining how warm she would be if she shared her blanket with Ian.

"Is something wrong, lass?" Michael asked.

"Uh, no. I'm fine. It's just going to be a cold night, is all."

"Aye, there will be a nip in the air, but what a beautiful sky." He stretched out by the small fire Ian had made and said no more.

"Yeah, beautiful," she sighed. It really stunk that she was freezing her butt off and didn't at least get to see the stars.

Ian said he didn't wish to draw too much attention

with a large fire, but Jenny's chattering teeth must have changed his mind and he threw another log onto the red coals. She huddled as close as she dared to the dancing flames, the tartan wrapped around her.

So much had happened to her in the last few days. Her mind raced over them all, but inevitably ended where they shouldn't. On Ian Southernland. To want a man like him was the worst thing she could do to herself, but she feared she no longer had any control over her feelings. As if she ever did.

Exhaustion found her as it did every night since she'd arrived in this time, and she fell asleep huddled beside the meager flames while dangerous thoughts, silly wishes, and sensuous fantasies filled her dreams.

Ian watched her closely, noting the sparks dancing in her eyes as she stared into the flames before sleep took her. She was a brave, beautiful woman, and for the life of him he couldn't stop the crushing need to have her. Michael was right, he should leave her well alone, and would.

Tomorrow he would push them hard to Edinburgh and he would find those blasted spectacles and get her back where she belonged. Safely in Colin's keep where solid stone walls separated them.

"Is it warm where she and Tuck come from?" Michael asked. "I've ne'er seen a lass so bothered by a slight chill."

"Aye, in part of their country," he said, recalling much of what Amelia had told him. "But she is unaccustomed to sleeping outside."

"I ken she didna travel much."

"Nay, she did not travel as Amelia." She hid away from the world. But why? Was there some wretch who had mistreated her? Or was she afraid all men were like her father, clearly without a heart. Why else would the man have let his only daughter wander through Scotland and beyond while threats for her safety had been laid at his feet? How could he not treasure her?

Jenny shivered and clutched the tartan tighter. Tomorrow he would put more distance between them, but he could not in good conscience allow the woman to freeze.

Knowing he tempted his sanity, he rose from his spot across from the meager flames and lay down beside her, ignoring Michael's knowing look. He pulled her into his arms then covered them with his blanket. She sighed softly against his neck and her shivering ceased.

Michael rolled to his side and pinned him with a look. "'Tis no' like you tae play with a lassie's heart."

Ian looked to the stars, but didn't relinquish his hold on her. "You said so yourself, she is frail. 'Tis for warmth, nothing more," he lied, to Michael and to himself.

"Are you goin' tae tell the lass of your false marriage afore we reach Edinburgh?" Michael asked, returning his attention to the star-speckled canvas above them. "'Twould be best if she didna hear it from your mouth in company. 'Twould ruin the tale."

"Aye, in the morning." And she would argue quite long upon the subject right after slapping him soundly for finding herself in his arms.

"At the inn, will you no' be expected tae share a room?"

"I will sleep outside her door. We will take turns, you and I," Ian said.

"I can only hope. I've grown tae like the lass, and wouldna' care tae have tae defend her honor," Michael said, no jest present in his voice whatsoever.

"You shall not have to. Now go to sleep."

Jenny murmured softly in her sleep, and Ian's treacherous ears swore she'd said his name. He fell asleep with a grin on his lips and dread in his heart. How was he going to maintain his honor and her virtue when an invisible force continued to push him closer to her with each passing hour?

****

Jenny felt warm, safe, and very comfortable. So much so she didn't want to open her eyes. That is until her pillow moved.

She fell very still and lifted her lids. A chin with a rather strong looking jaw covered in a day old fair-haired beard was barely a breath away from her face. This close she had no trouble seeing the slight cleft faintly hidden beneath the stubble.

With a gulp she lifted her head, dying to get a really good look at Ian Southernland. Without her glasses she had to be nearly nose-to-nose with the man to see him, and this was her only chance, because she didn't believe for one minute that they would find a peddler with glasses, least of all one with any strong enough to make much of a difference. Regardless of how many wishes she made.

Praying Ian was still sound asleep, his deep breathing hinting that he was, she let her gaze travel along his powerful jaw across his features. She was stunned, awed, and thoroughly amazed at how right Tuck had been. He was the very image of her Prince Charming. He was beautiful.

There was a hitch in his breathing and she suddenly found a pair of startling blue eyes peering back at her. She licked her lips as she struggled for something coherent to say while her limbs had locked in place, but what? Sorry I slept on you?

Those amazing eyes darkened, sending her good sense to the farthest edge of the planet, and she pressed her mouth to his. He was not appalled by her actions, quite the opposite. Like a whisper, he teased and tormented her with his lips, warm and soft, and full of sin.

She should stop this. This wasn't a good idea, for either of them. But he ignored the faint sound in the back of her throat and took complete advantage of her unintelligible protest, if that's what one would call it. She wasn't so sure any longer. Perhaps more of a moan, if she examined it more closely. But examinations were the furthest thing from her mind.

Sliding his hand to the back of her head, he held her captive as he invaded the inner recesses of her mouth, exploring, tasting, devouring. So much more than the kiss they'd first shared. This one held more fire, more power, more—*wow*.

Michael stirred.

What was she doing? She scrambled off Ian's chest to a safe distance. What to say? How to make herself say that it could never happen again when all she wanted was for it to happen over and over and over?

"I'm sorry," she managed to squeak out.

Ian sat up and propped his arm on a bended knee with a sigh. "So am I, little one. So am I." He got to his feet and started breaking camp.

She let her gaze drop from his powerful form to the ground beneath her. Sorry? Yeah, she could well imagine he was sorry. Kissing the irritating scientist. Yeah, right, big mistake.

"Why am I not surprised?" she mumbled as she got to her feet. She wasn't the type he usually dallied with, of that she was certain. Even she could tell he preferred the Innes's of the world. Tall, shapely...giggly. Cinderella wannabe's were not for him.

After a quick bite to eat, one she didn't taste, they set out for Edinburgh, Ian on his horse and Jenny on hers. She sighed at the blurry sight of his broad shoulders. Well, she supposed it was for the best. Knowing he wasn't interested in her early on was better than a much more humiliating turndown later.

Her hand slipped from the pommel to her lips. But why did he kiss her if he wasn't interested?

****

Idiot, dolt, fool! Ian called himself that and more. He'd meant to arise before her, not let her find herself in his arms. Mostly to save her any embarrassment and him a firm slap to the face. But nay, she had not slapped him, not physically. Her stammered apology was more than enough. She did not want him, not in truth.

Ah, but that kiss. He couldn't recall anything so sweet, so inviting, so painfully arousing as the warmth of her tongue sparing with his, her small lithe body curled against him, those lily white legs tangling with his beneath the blanket.

He shifted in his saddle at the sudden discomfort. He had to banish the memory from his mind. She did not, could not want him. It was nothing more than a bit of curiosity on her part, no doubt. An accident, as it were. His brow furrowed. Was she experimenting on him in some way?

Michael cleared his throat and nodded toward their charge.

Ah yes. His lie. He would return to his musings over the true reason she kissed him at a later time. "Mistress Maxwell, there is aught something I must tell you."

She cut her eyes at him, but would not look directly

at him. Puzzling. If they're encounter had been an experiment, would she not be more inclined to observe his reactions for some time? Or had that kiss been the result of something else?

He shifted his thoughts back to his announcement and continued. "For your safety, I have decided to let it be known that I have taken you to wife."

She snapped her head around and narrowed her eyes at him. "That is absolutely ridiculous."

That certainly got her attention. But as he had feared, she argued against his decision for nigh on to three hours.

"I don't see why we have to lie," she said for the seventh or possibly the eighth time. He'd lost count as they plodded along the road.

And for the seventh or eighth time, he said, "'Twill make life simpler and safer if we do so."

"No one has bothered us—*me* since that first day."

Having had quite enough of the entire debate, Ian pulled his horse alongside hers, reached over, plucked her from the saddle, and planted her firmly in front of him.

"You're not going to win this argument by picking me up like a sack of potatoes," she snarled.

With a chuckle, he said, "Sweeting, there is no argument. I have made my decision and it shall stand. Now, I suggest you hold on."

He kicked his mount into a steady gallop with Michael shaking his head as they sped past. The sooner he got her to an inn and out of his sight the better it would be for them all.

Of course he was having the devil of a time with her wrapped around him at present, but with a destination ahead of them, and perhaps a bit of peace, he was more than willing to endure it.

He may even leave her in Michael's care this evening and find himself some true relief. That would surely get his mind off of her and that tantalizing kiss. And more importantly, the search for a reason behind it. He did not wish to think she wanted him, for it would try his resolve to remain at arm's length from the woman.

After an endless ride, he slowed his mount and felt her fingers loosen their death grip on his doublet.

"I wish you wouldn't do that," she muttered.

"'Twas necessary. If you will but look, we have arrived."

And none too soon. Jenny felt the rapid beat of her heart, and knew it wasn't from fear. The ride had excited her in many ways, none of them good. Or all of them good, she supposed it really had to do with one's perspective. In any event, she was glad they'd arrived, and she could put some well-needed space between her and Ian's wonderfully broad, warm chest.

Within an hour they had rooms at an inn, one Ian had apparently frequented before, and Jenny was enjoying her first hot bath in days. Although she did have to endure spiteful muttered words from the maids and the raucous comments made by the innkeeper, Mr. Dougal, about their marriage. Still a bath was a bath, and she savored it.

She giggled as she rinsed her hair. Recalling some of the things said to Ian about his recent nuptials and some of the comments made by the girls. It served him right if his love life had taken a distinct nosedive. She'd tried to tell him it wasn't necessary, had some very fine points in her favor, but he wouldn't listen, the stubborn oaf.

The water turned cool, and she climbed from the tub and got dressed. All the while, she struggled to keep images of Ian's sleepy warm gaze from her mind. If they really were married, she could look at those eyes every morning and more.

"No. That won't ever happen." They probably wouldn't even sleep in the same bed. Separate accommodations were common for a husband and wife of his station in this century. And he'd probably have a mistress somewhere that he'd rather spend his nights with. He was a rogue, after all.

"What am I thinking? The man would never even consider me," she said with a snort. Her fantasies were clouding her brain. She had to get a grip on reality.

While drying her hair by the fire there was a knock at the door.

"Come in," she called.

"I—" Ian cleared his throat and clasped his hands behind his back, and stood rooted to the spot. It was that or lunge across the space in a breath and bury his hands and face in the long damp tresses. "I came to see if you were ready to dine."

"Yes, I'm starved." She stood, and pulled her hair back with a ribbon.

He crossed the room in two strides and took the satin from her fingers and tied a bow. The slope of her neck begged to be kissed. He swallowed the need before it consumed him. Torturing himself, he allowed his fingers to trail down the length of her hair before stepping away.

"Um, thank you," she said, her voice somewhat unsteady.

Could it be that she wanted him in truth? That she'd not been performing some sort of research?

"My pleasure." He took her hand and secured it in the crook of his arm, then guided her downstairs. If she did want him, then he was a man in dire trouble, for how could he possibly refuse her?

Dinner was actually a pleasant affair, Jenny noted. She hadn't expected to enjoy herself so much, but Michael had finally stopped his incessant chatter about Fiona, and Ian had managed to not start a single argument with her since they left her room. He barely spoke, to be exact. She decided not to investigate the reasons for his silence, and listened to Michael recount tales of the many tangles Ian and Colin had gotten into on their trips across the country.

At one point she found herself laughing so hard she nearly snorted wine through her nose. Not a ladylike thing to do, but then Mr. Dougal had supplied them with so much of the stuff, she found herself rather tipsy.

Swiping tears from her eyes, she said, "I don't believe that story for a minute, but I loved it, just the same."

"I've only told what Colin himself has said," Michael said, but Jenny knew he had to be wearing a huge grin.

Ian chuckled. "By the time it was told to you, whelp, it had already grown to such gargantuan proportion, that no one could believe it."

"You have a knack for tales, Michael," Jenny said. "Thanks for sharing them. But," she said, quickly covering a yawn. "I think I've had too much wine and should probably be getting to bed."

Ian rose and pulled out her chair. "Michael, you shall take second watch," he said. Taking her hand, he escorted her from the room.

"Second watch?" she asked, as they climbed the stairs.

"One of us shall be standing guard outside your door through the night," Ian said, opening her bedroom door.

"But that's—"

"You will not know we are here, but if you should need anything, one of us shall be but a few steps away."

He pushed her inside and closed the door before she could argue. "Oh, this is ridiculous," she grumbled.

"But necessary," she heard him say through the door.

"Fine. Torture yourself on the floor," she said with a huff, and readied herself for bed.

It only took a few minutes before guilt gnawed at her. Ian was going to spend half the long cold night on the floor outside her room. It was unheard of, ridiculous, and completely unfair. He had ridden just as hard as she. Oh, sure she was new at it, but he had to be tired, longing for a real bed, just as much as she did. And it was her fault. He didn't want her to come along, and now she was his responsibility.

"More like an albatross," she muttered, disgusted with herself for bringing all this about. If she'd just not run from him that first night...

A boisterous laugh echoed in the hallway. "Och, doona say she's thrown ye out, lad!"

"Oh no," she moaned. Now he was to be humiliated too? His unwilling bride had tossed the infamous rogue out of his own bed.

Jenny chewed the inside of her cheek, trying hard not to laugh. Well, he probably deserved it for one of his many seedy liaisons in the past. But it did seem a bit unfair since he was only trying to protect her.

An idea bloomed and with a nod she stumbled across the room to the door. Flinging it wide, she froze at the sight of the small crowd gathering in the hall. Maids, the innkeeper's wife, even Michael, or so she thought, as she squinted at the group. But she would not be deterred. At least she could still tell which one was Ian. He was the only tall, blonde, broad shouldered man among them.

She threw her arms around his neck. "Darling! I'm so sorry. I didn't mean it." He stumbled into the room and grasped her waist for balance bringing him close, very close. Close enough she could actually see him. She attempted to resist the urge to sigh with pleasure, but failed. She could only hope he hadn't heard it with all the noise in the hallway.

"Well, lad, kiss the lass. 'Tis the only way tae make up after a spat," Mr. Dougal said.

"Yes, that, um, is the custom," she said, knowing she'd hate herself for it later. The man didn't want her, but she wanted him in more ways than she thought humanly possible.

"Aye, 'tis the only way," Ian murmured. His lips brushed hers with the softest of touches sending tingles down her back and along her arms. It wasn't a wow kiss like the others, this one was different. Sweeter than any sugar—or sugar replacement—she'd ever tasted.

"Och, now there's a fine sight," the innkeeper's wife said. "Let the lover's be, dear. Come tae bed."

"Aye, a fine sight indeed," Mr. Dougal said, and the door clicked closed.

They were alone, and Ian was still kissing her. Oh how she wanted it to be real, but the truth of it brought her to her senses and she pulled back. "I'm sorry. I was only trying to—they were—you were—"

She planted her hands on her hips. "I couldn't sleep with all that racket." She spun away after spouting out that whopper and climbed into bed. "You do what you want. I'm going to bed." And cry myself to sleep, she thought.

Ian stared, his arms painfully empty, as she covered her beautiful body with a pile of quilts and laid her head and all that long hair on the pillow. Her chemise was nearly see-through, a fact he was certain she was unaware of, considering her lack of spectacles, and to feel all of her pressed against him had gone straight to his head…and other regions of his person.

He was thankful he'd been the one directly in front of the door when she'd thrown it open. All those elegant curves had been made visible by the firelight from behind her, and when she'd grabbed him, he was lost.

She sighed softly, and he had no doubt that she'd fallen asleep. The woman could drop off at the slightest whim.

A grin stole over his mouth. She couldn't sleep because of the noise? Hardly. The lady felt sorry for him. She cared, in a way, but it warmed him further, which was not good.

He took a deep breath, turned from the temptation to climb into her bed and find out for certain what her feelings were, then went back into the hallway to stand guard.

Michael was there waiting with a frown on his face. "Glad I am tae see you didna stay abed."

He gave the lad his sternest glare. "She is a lady."

"Who has no' sense in her head where you're concerned."

Ian narrowed his gaze. "She was merely trying to save face."

He chuckled with a shake of his head. "Aye, you keep tellin' yourself that one." He strolled down the hall to their assigned room and slipped through the door.

Chapter Eight

The day came too early for Ian, but he mustered himself and made his way down the hall to Jenny's room. Michael stood as he approached.

"Is the lady awake?" he asked.

"Aye, she's been rustlin' around in there for several minutes."

Ian nodded and turned to knock on the door.

"Just a minute," Jenny said. With more scuffling, and a faint muttered curse, she opened the door. "Good morning."

Ian couldn't withhold his smile at the sight of her bright cheery face. She seemed to have slept well, and yet, there were faint circles under her eyes. He wondered if she spent the night tossing and turning as much as he did once he traded watch with Michael.

But no, she was sleeping soundly when he left last night. 'Twas likely her worry over finding a pair of spectacles and the need for much more rest after their journey. She wasn't used to such things.

"Are you ready for some nourishment, mistress?" he asked.

"Absolutely."

He placed her hand on his arm and escorted her to the dining room. The three of them had a quiet meal and discussed their plans for the day. Dougal didn't know of a peddler, but directed them to a shopkeeper not too far away that might know of such a man.

"I will go and see what he knows. The two of you stay here until I return," Ian said, and was promptly rebuked.

"Not on your life. I'm going with you. I didn't come all this way to be stuck in here while you do all the hunting. I want to experience what I can while I'm here. And you need me to pick out the glasses."

"And I didna come all this way tae go home empty-handed. I'll need me gift for Fiona. Perhaps this shop will have the verra thing I need," Michael said.

He sighed. "Fine, I am far too tired to bicker with the two of you."

Michael and Jenny turned to one another and chatted on about the things Fiona might like. A conversation Ian felt compelled to stay out of, but knew full well all the girl wanted was a ring. Still he kept his mouth shut then gulped down the last of his tea.

"Let us be off," he said, and rose, taking Jenny's hand without thinking. It was becoming habit, he supposed, since the girl couldn't see and needed aid. But he was enjoying it far too much.

They made their way down the street, while Jenny pestered them with question after question. He chuckled at her inquisitiveness, the scientist in her wanting to know everything, the girl in her thrilled with the adventure. He no longer thought she would hide in her laboratory once she returned home. She had changed in the short time he'd known her. Her very words, *I want to experience what I can*, proved him correct. And although she was still the most inquisitive, talkative woman he had ever known, she was also the most alive and vibrant. He was going to miss her when she left.

Shaking off the uncomfortable thought, he guided his little group into the shop Dougal had told them about.

"I doona know of a peddler, but I have a few of them fancy spectacles, if you'd like tae see them," the shopkeeper said.

"Oh, could we? That would be wonderful," Jenny said, her eyes wide with wonder and delight.

Ian knew she'd truly believed they wouldn't find a single pair of the things. He wanted to gloat, but could only smile instead. She looked so charming trying on the horrid things and blinking owlishly at him.

It was obvious she couldn't see any better with them than without. He hated the disappointment he read in her face.

He slipped his arm around her waist and squeezed her tight against his side. "We are not yet done, little one," he said softly in her ear. "The peddler will have more to choose from."

"Yes," she said, nodding with a forced smile. "Of course. Thank you, sir, for letting me see your fine assortment of spectacles." She stepped out of Ian's grasp and handed over the last pair.

"Jenny, what do you think of this?" Michael said, holding up a ring.

She shook her head with a crooked grin. "You know I can't see it."

The young man smiled sheepishly. "Sorry, lass. I keep forgettin'. But 'tis a ring, like you said she might be wantin', I think."

"Oh? Here, let me have it," she said, holding out her hand. She lifted it the tip of her nose and ran her fingers over it carefully. "These inscriptions, what are they? I can't see the detail."

"Celt inscriptions. It reminds me of Tuck's ring. Do you no' think she'll like it? Should I no' get one like hers?"

As the two talked of Fiona and her likes and dislikes, Ian could only stare at Jenny. She had said when she was very close to something she could see it, but he hadn't really understood until now the limits she suffered. He had to find her those bloody spectacles. He would search every shop, every peddler's cart, he'd go as far as London if need be. But he would not fail her in this.

He paused in his musings and wondered where this intense desire for her and for her happiness came from. It was nothing like he'd ever experienced before. He wasn't sure he cared for the feeling.

"You need to choose a ring that makes you think of her. When you hold this," Jenny said to Michael, "who or what do you think of?"

The young Scot laughed. "I think of the money it costs, not my Fiona. I'm beginnin' tae understand."

"Finally!" Ian laughed, forcing himself into the conversation and safely away from his own thoughts. "That alone will be the greatest gift the young lady shall receive upon our return."

Jenny laughed but swatted his arm. "Stop teasing him, Ian."

He snatched the offending hand and pressed a kiss to it before he could stop himself. Her stunned expression then shy smile added to this strange feeling growing inside him. Aye, his future was looking quite grim indeed.

"Come my friends, we need to find those elusive spectacles." And he needed to complete this trip as soon as possible before it was too late.

He thanked the shopkeeper for his help and the three of them strolled out of the establishment and down the street.

Jenny eyed her hand and Ian's where it sat firmly atop hers on his arm. It was silly, she knew that, but no one had ever kissed her hand before. Somehow it felt more intimate than the kisses they'd already shared.

I step through one little time portal and my entire way of thinking is skewed. There must be a correlation.

And there was. And he had a name. Ian Southernland.

She sighed silently and continued on toward the next shop. All her life she'd tried to get her father's attention without success. Now here she was, walking alongside a man whose attention she wanted in so many ways, on so many levels, she couldn't catalog them all. But she refused to make the same mistakes she had with her father. She wouldn't change herself to be what he wanted, not this time.

Jenny cleared her throat to cover her cheerless laugh. As if she could suddenly become a beautiful, voluptuous, alluring woman. Not even a fairy godmother could pull that one off. No, she would have to be content with what they were. Friends.

A smile slipped over her lips with the thought. Yes, they were friends. Although they argued regularly about almost everything, it was a companionable sort of discourse. One she rather enjoyed. And there was so much more behind Ian's beautiful face and perfect body. He possessed a keen mind and a desire to know more, traits she greatly admired, and she would never find a more desirable man in her life.

But friends they were, and friends they would remain. She liked the attention he gave her, no longer feeling it was just because of his vow to protect her. There was more to it. That gentle squeeze in the shop when none of the glasses worked. The compliments he gave her even though he didn't want her in bed. The way he took her hand and guided her along the cobblestones without thinking twice. Yes, she could live with just being friends. After all, it was far more than she had before she came here.

****

Hours and a dozen shops and peddlers later, they returned to the inn with only one happy soul. Michael had found what he was seeking, and Fiona would be very pleased. But Jenny had not found a single pair of glasses worth keeping. She wouldn't, however, let her disappointment show. She refused to ruin Michael's joy.

He babbled on about his *sweet lass* and how much she'd love the ring he found for her, and his eagerness to return home now that he found it.

"Och, but I wasna' thinkin'. I'm sorry, Jenny," he said. "I know you're disappointed that we didna find your spectacles, but I know we will. Tomorrow, 'tis certain."

She smiled at him and rose from the dinner table. "Thank you, Michael. I'm sure we will. If you gentleman will excuse me, I'm very tired." They both rose and Ian took her hand. "No, stay. Finish your meal. I'll be fine from here to my room. No one will bother me."

Ian bowed over her hand and pressed a small kiss. "Goodnight, little one."

She disappeared into the hallway and felt along the wall and found the stair. The innkeeper's wife happened to be coming down and took Jenny's hand and led her to her room. While she chattered away, Jenny put Ian's chivalry from her mind. They were friends, she reminded herself. And it served no purpose to dwell on kisses and such. She had glasses to find, twins to deliver, and a life to return to in the twenty-first century. One she knew would be empty without Ian in it.

****

The next day they set out again in search of the peddler. He was known, according to one shopkeeper, to frequent a local spot that was a bit too seedy for Jenny. With her sputtering and muttering her arguments, Michael hauled her back to the inn while Ian went in search of the man.

As he entered the pub, Ian thought of Jenny and her flushed face as Michael towed her off. He would get a sore tongue lashing upon his return, but he grinned nevertheless.

It didn't take him long to locate the peddler, but he was deep in his cups and his wares safely locked away. Ian did manage to get the man to agree to meet at the inn the following morning after several rounds, all supplied by Ian. He only hoped the sod remembered when he woke the next morn with what would be a formidable headache. Ian would not fair well either. What had possessed him to partake so much? He knew the answer before he finished the thought.

Jenny.

"I am losing my mind," he muttered. Perhaps he should seek someone, a fair someone to help him overcome these odd feelings he had for the woman.

The bar maid had been trying to catch his eye most of the evening. Why not accept what she so obviously offered?

It took naught but a wink and a smile to have her sitting on his lap. She slipped her fingers into his hair and whispered tantalizing things in his ear. Strange, he thought, how her fingers didn't feel nearly as nice as Jenny's. And her body didn't fit against his, although she was more like the sort he fancied. Buxom, well rounded, willing, and...temporary. But for the life of him, he couldn't seem to stir the least bit of interest in the chit.

He ordered them both another drink and hoped, after downing the contents, that the very detailed images she was painting in his mind would bring about some change. But alas, no. He could only see a woman with long brown hair and a fey-like smile.

With a resigned sigh, he placed his cup on the table. "My dear, if we had but met a few days ago I would gladly accompany you to your room, but I fear I am needed elsewhere this eve." He took her hand, dirty though it was, and pressed a kiss to the back, then quickly left the maid behind.

His thoughts plagued him as he made his way back to the inn. To lust after a woman was one thing, but to lust after *only* one was quite another. It boggled the mind. How could a man such as he, with no heart ties to anyone but a few friends and his half-sister feel the inexplicable

97

urge to claim one woman as his own?

He paused before the inn and looked up at the lights in the windows. The one woman he could not have, did not want to want, plagued him. She was stubborn, argumentative, even shrewish at times, and she thought him to be stubborn, officious, arrogant, and a fool. That last cut most deeply, for when it came down to it, she saw him as so many did, an empty-headed skirt chasing rogue. His many slights, although not intentional were proof enough.

Well, he would admit to his success with the ladies, but he never did the chasing. They always came to him, with a few rare exceptions. She, however, was not of a mind to chase him. And he could not, in good conscience, chase her. She was a lady and he would not spoil her for his own pleasures.

Ah, but who will be doing the leaving when all is done? A voice whispered in his ear. She was of a mind to return home to her own time, leaving him here in the past.

"Nay," he muttered with a shake of his head. The ending does not make it right. And after all, she did not want him. Twice now she apologized for kissing him. Not something a woman would say if she were interested. But would he stop wanting her, needing her once she left?

"Need her? Bloody hell. Another drink is what I need," he grumbled, and with a slight sway to his gait, made his way inside. With luck, it would drive away the disturbing feeling brushing against his heart.

"There you are, Ian. I was about tae come lookin' for you," Michael said.

Jenny appeared by his side. "Did you find him? Did you see any of the glasses? Did you bring any back with you?"

"Aye and nay." Ian let out a long sigh and cast a wavering gaze on Michael. "Lad, would you be kind enough to fetch me a drink. I am in need of it."

"Well?" Jenny prodded as Michael turned away with a confused frown on his face.

"I met with the man and he assured me he had many spectacles for you to choose from. He will be here on the morrow."

"Why didn't he just come back with you?"

Ian took the drink from Michael's hand and downed nearly all of it at once. Jenny jostled his arm, making it run around his lips and down his neck, but he didn't care. He needed it after seeing her pretty face alight with hope and excitement. He'd wanted to throw her over his shoulder, take to the stairs three at a time, and go straight to her room and her bed. He should've at least tried to relieve his stress with the pretty maid at the pub, but he knew it for the lie that it was. His desire, his need burned for one woman at present.

"Ian, would you please stop guzzling that stuff and answer me," she snipped.

He lowered the empty cup and handed it to Michael for a refill. "If you please." He then turned to the beautiful woman by his side, with a face as red as a fire poker. She started to speak once more, and he quickly placed his finger against her lips, enjoying the warm moist feel of them, while damning his bad luck at the same time.

"The peddler was deep in his cups at the time," he said. "Even if he could have accompanied me here, he would have chosen not to."

Michael appeared, thank heaven, with another drink, and Ian removed his finger from her luscious lips before he made a complete ass of himself and replaced his finger with his mouth. The thought urged him to empty the cup, post haste, which he did. It was that or slip his hand around her pretty neck and pull her against him for a most desired kiss.

"Are you drunk?" she asked.

"I believe I am, sweeting."

"Jenny, lass, I think 'tis a good time for you tae be going tae bed," Michael said.

"But—"

"Now, lass," Michael said, his voice low and firm. Highly unusual, but it seemed to have the desired effect.

In a swirl of skirts and a pout so delicious Ian was tempted to follow her, Jenny stomped up the stairs.

"I would love to know how you managed that, my lad," Ian said, in complete wonder and silently thrilled and disappointed that he'd not acted on his thoughts.

"A firm hand. 'Tis all a woman needs."

Ian let out a chortle with that one. "This from the man who was laid on his back in no less than a breath by Amelia Tucker?" He dropped his hand on the lad's shoulder. "And had to face his intended's wrath over her desire to learn how to do the same?"

"'Tis different. Jenny isna as strong as my Fiona, nor Tuck. And you are clearly no' in any condition for polite company."

"Ah, yes. Ladies do not care to be around men when they drink."

"You mean when they're drunk. There's a difference, mon. Care tae tell me why?"

"Nay. But now that I am quite thoroughly soused, I think I shall retire for the evening. You take first watch."

"Aye, but I doona think you'll be awake for the second."

Ian looked back over his shoulder as he gripped the handrail. "I will do my part. I made a vow to protect her." He turned back to the stair. "Even from myself."

****

The sounds of the world going about its daily business outside his window brought Ian out of a dreamless sleep. With a moan, most pitiful, he grabbed his head and stumbled out of bed. He paused in his misery and grappled with his memories. He had failed in his duty to guard Jenny. Michael had been forced to sit watch all night.

Cursing his stupidity the eve before and his current sorry state, he dressed. He owed Michael an apology.

"Och, so he lives," the lad said as he entered the room.

"'Tis a matter of opinion."

Michael chuckled, raking across Ian's tattered nerves.

With a hiss of pain, he straightened and turned to his tormentor, his finger at his lips.

"You are in a sorry state," Michael said lowly. "But tae ease your pain, you doona have tae rise. You can sleep the day away. I will take care of Jenny."

"Nay," he said with more force than he thought he possessed. "I made a vow. I cannot express how deeply I regret my actions." He crossed to the basin and poured a goodly amount of water into the bowl and splashed it onto his face. Lifting his head, he grimaced at the haggard man looking back at him in the mirror.

Michael chuckled and crossed his arms. "Aye, but you're paying for them now." He dropped his arms, his smile fading. "She was and is safe."

He dried his face and hands and turned from his sorry reflection. "I left you to do my duty. That was poorly done. I owe you an apology, lad." He bent to retrieve his boots while praying his brain remained inside his skull.

"Verra well. Apology accepted. But you doona have tae rise. The lass has met with the peddler and is somewhat happy with her new eyes."

Ian's head snapped up and he winced. "She can see?"

"No' as well as she would like, but, aye, she is no' blind any longer." He chuckled low. "And I think 'tis best if she no' see you like this. You willna survive her haranguing. She isna a lass tae tread kindly on a mon in a state such as yours, I'm thinkin'."

"Nay, she will not be kind, I am certain. But I have a feeling she will carryon no matter the time I arise. 'Twould be best to get it over with."

He shoved his feet into his boots and followed Michael out the door and downstairs. He didn't fear Jenny's sharp tongue, although it would be most painful. It was her reaction to seeing him for the first time that concerned him. He knew, deep in his heart, she would not swoon, as some maids had done in the past. But would she at least care for his form?

And what do I care if she does?

Care, there was that dreadful word again. How could he care for the woman when they'd known one another for barely more than a sennight? They had been thrown together on this journey, talked of many things, argued over most, but somehow he'd come to care for her. He suddenly wished he'd not made such a hasty decision to face her so soon.

Jenny turned at the sound of boots on the stairs, more curious than ever to see with her somewhat adjusted vision Ian Southernland for the first time from head to toe. She couldn't see as well as she would like, but she wouldn't bump into furniture and trees any more.

That was a blessing. But seeing the man who could kiss like nobody's business, would that be a blessing or a curse?

Seeing Michael had been a surprise. The way he spoke, often made her think of him as a very young man, more a gangly youth, but the reality was quite the opposite. He was young in years, yes, possibly not even twenty, but he was old in so many other ways. He was broad, big, and had his share of scars and a slightly crooked nose, but he was pure Highlander Warrior. No wonder Fiona spoke so breathlessly about him.

A smile teased the edge of her lips as she thought of where the man had obtained that crooked nose. Tuck had clocked him once when she first came to this time, but the young man had no ill feelings toward her. Admiration and respect flowed from him whenever he spoke of Tuck.

Thinking of Tuck made Jenny think of her friend's husband, Colin. If Michael looked so wonderfully male, then Colin must be a true sight to see. She could hardly wait to get back to Arreyder Castle and see him and Tuck and everyone else.

But Ian. Seeing him would be the most difficult.

Michael was the first to emerge from the stairway, a broad grin on his handsome face. She smiled tremulously as he stepped to the side and she saw Ian Southernland for the first time.

Blinking, she stared at the man, her heart hammering so loud the sounds of the inn and the bustle outside were drowned out. She'd known he was beautiful, she'd seen him up close and caught glimpses of his handsome profile whenever he saw fit to pick her up. But the whole man, all that gorgeous testosterone standing before her, left her utterly breathless.

"Hello," she said, her voice barely a whisper. She swallowed, attempting to remove the sudden dryness from her mouth.

He cocked his head a bit and bowed. "Good morning, mistress. I hope you had a pleasant rest?"

Knees weak from the doubly dangerous combination of his voice and form, she found a nearby chair and sank into it. "Yes," she croaked.

Heaven help her. If she had seen him, really seen

him that first night they met, she would've fallen into his arms and begged him to take her anywhere with him.

"I am glad you suffered no ill will from my failure to guard you last eve," he said, moving to stand before her.

She shook her head, lost in those incredible blue eyes, although red from his binge, they still held her firmly in awe.

He motioned toward her face, and she noted his long elegant fingers. Callused, she was sure, but the thought of what those hands could do for a woman sent a shiver through her.

"These spectacles are sufficient?" he asked.

"Um, yes. I can see fairly well."

He chuckled, the spread of his full lips exposing white straight teeth. "You will admit then, that I was correct?" A dimple appeared in one freshly shaved cheek, and she ached to run her finger over the small crescent shape.

"What? Oh, you mean in finding me some glasses." She closed her eyes for a moment to regain her composure. He was too much for a pair of hungry eyes such as hers. She needed to take him in a little at a time.

"Yes, I will concede that I believed we'd not find a single pair. And although they are crude in their design, they accomplish the basic task." She lifted her lids to find him smiling down at her.

"I will be a gentleman and not gloat," he said with a wink, then turned toward one of the maids and ordered some food. He sat beside her at the small table while Michael sat across from her.

How dare he flirt with her after stumbling in drunk and smelling of something she dare not describe? Had he spent the evening with a woman after dealing with the peddler? The little man who'd sold her the glasses could barely remember what happened the night before. She'd questioned him thoroughly on the subject, but all he could recall was a gentleman telling him to be at Dougal's Inn in the morning.

Why had Ian gotten drunk? The question tumbled over and over in her mind for hours last night as she struggled to fall asleep. More to the point, was the woman pretty?

She nearly growled aloud at her ridiculous thoughts. He wasn't attracted to her. He was a rogue, a ladies' man. A kiss meant nothing to him. Nothing at all. There were logical reasons for each incident, she assured herself. Not a single kiss had been real, only tools, weapons, a means to an end.

"Since 'tis too late in the day to begin our journey back to Arreyder Castle, what say we venture through the town? I myself would like to visit a gentleman I have heard tell of who deals in horseflesh."

Ian cast a smile at her and her breath hitched.

"I shall wager you would like to see as much as you can before retuning. Is that not so?" he asked.

She cleared her throat and her unruly thoughts from her mind as she adjusted her glasses. "Yes, I would like to see some of Edinburgh before we leave." But Ian Southernland and his kisses wove through her mind like an intricate tapestry with hidden pictures, ones she had to find, if only to put her hopeful heart, her silly Cinderella dreams to rest.

"Then 'tis settled. We shall go out. What say you?"

Ian's cheery demeanor, forced and pained as his pounding head reminded him, seemed his only recourse in dealing with Jenny. He hoped those probing brown eyes of hers would cease their study of him and soon. Sitting beside her at the table, he could see the rapid pulse at her throat.

She found him pleasing to the eye, and perhaps more. A fact that bothered him on many levels. How was he to maintain what little sanity he still possessed if she continued to look at him in such a way? Their outing would be painful to his aching head, but a needed distraction. With her preoccupation with the town, perhaps he would refrain from pulling her into his arms and devouring her sweet mouth.

Michael took up the conversation as Ian ate his late morning meal, one he prayed would stay down. Apparently Dougal and his wife had an inkling of his condition and served him bread and broth instead of the spicier dishes he was accustomed to.

"Mary, thank Mrs. Dougal for me. The meal was delicious as always," he said to the maid as she took his now empty bowl. She giggled and scurried back to the kitchen. Ian ignored Jenny's narrowed gaze. Best to think she was put out with his behavior last night rather than jealous over the girl.

"Shall we be off?" he said, rising to his feet, feeling steadier than before. Perhaps the day wouldn't be as painful as he thought.

Chapter Nine

The day was bright as they strolled along the street and through the shops. Jenny bubbled with such wonder, Ian could do naught but watch her. The many envious stares cast his way, made his chest swell, and his heart sink. She was not his. His hope that the afternoon would prove to be less painful than when he awoke with his aching head had vanished nearly the moment he'd had the ludicrous thought.

He would resist her, all of her. He had no choice. She was a lady, and although she seemed attracted to him, he would not pursue a liaison with her.

They went back to the shop they'd entered that first day. The ring Michael had looked at caught Jenny's eye and Ian knew she wanted it. But she refused to spend her limited funds on the thing. She said she was saving the money Tuck had given her for presents for the babies.

Ian admired her decision, but would not let her leave without the ring, so he purchased it for her against her rather loud protests. But he could see the delight in her eyes even while she argued with him.

"I don't have to have it," she complained.

"What is a pretty lady without a pretty bobble?" he asked, pulling out some coins.

"But it's so expensive. I know a good deal about the economy here. You are not going to buy it for me."

"I most certainly am." He slipped it on her finger before she could protest. "You see, 'tis a perfect fit." He handed the shopkeeper the coins and thanked him.

"But, Ian—"

He gripped her shoulders and looked into her wide eyes. "'Tis my gift to you, little one. I wish for you to remember me when you return home," he said.

She smiled softly. "I could never forget you."

He brushed his finger across her cheek, resisting the

desire to kiss her. He knew it would take the last of his willpower and he would be lost. "Nor I you."

They left the store and found the man Ian had heard was a fine horse trader. He felt confident he would make some passing good deals with the fellow in the future, but had difficulty concentrating on much of anything with Jenny hesitantly wandering the stables, so he politely declined doing any business at the moment.

They wandered the city till nearly sunset before returning to the inn. Jenny bought all sorts of things, clothing mostly, an odd text here and there, but she was happy with her purchases.

After a quick bite they all retired early so they could get a decent night's rest before leaving at first light. Ian, however, wasn't happy with the way Jenny continued to look at him. Her eyes were nigh burning his skin. It was maddening!

He escorted her to her room and tossed the bundle of frippery she'd purchased on the bed. "Cease your constant examination of my form! Your eyes have plagued me from the moment you put on those bloody spectacles, and I cannot bear it any longer."

"I'm sorry. I didn't realize I was staring. I—you—it's just that—" She planted her fists on her hips. "Why did you kiss me?" Pacing across the floor, she shook her head. "I've gone over it and over it, but nothing computes. The first time was to create a distraction for the guards at the fountain," she said, ticking the incidents off on her fingers.

"The third was the same, to satisfy Mr. Dougal and the others that we were a happily married couple. But the second makes no sense whatsoever. Now that I can see you, really see you, I've been racking my brain over why. Your type is drawn to beautiful women, and beautiful women are drawn to you."

She crossed her arms and peered at him through those dreadful spectacles. "It simply isn't logical. I don't fit into that equation."

His irritation waned with her words. The woman had no inkling of her beauty or his overwhelming desire for her. It was a rare thing to find someone so utterly without artifice, and it made her all the more tempting.

"'Twas you who kissed me, sweeting," he said, hiding his grin.

"I did not!" He raised a brow at that blatant lie. "Well, maybe a little, but you took over," she said, shaking her finger at him. "You were in complete control. You could've stopped at any time. Now answer the question."

"No theories?"

"A few," she said with a curt nod. "At first I considered it to be an automatic response due to the proximity of our bodies, but I dismissed that, because you have shown a unique ability to ignore the overt advances made by that farm girl and others here at the inn. Regardless of the fact that you've told them we're married, it isn't true, so there should be no reason for you to not—you know," she said, waggling her fingers in the air. "But you haven't."

"Really? And you are certain of this?" This was a most interesting development. How could she not know how much he desired her? But it was to come to naught, he reminded himself.

Her gaze danced about the room, lighting on everything but him. "I asked Michael," she admitted beneath her breath.

Crossing his arms, he leaned back against the wall and watched her, fascinated by the shades of red flushing her pale skin. "Ah, well he is an honest man."

She jerked her head around, those large brown eyes framed by those horrid spectacles pinned him in place. "If you were in need of—if you needed to—"

"If I needed to what?" he asked, shamefully enjoying her consternation.

She lifted her chin at a jaunty angle. "You haven't answered my question."

"I am surprised you have yet to uncover the truth, as I know your mind to be quick. 'Tis verily simple," he chuckled.

"I don't find this humorous."

"Oh, but I do. I find it most humorous."

She threw up her arms and spun around. "Oh forget it. I've more important things to concentrate on other than—than—"

"Sex?"

She glared at him over her shoulder. "I was going to say, you." Yanking the items from the bundle, she grumbled. "You probably only kissed me because of some dream you were having. Likely about that farm girl or one of many others. An overactive imagination," she said, pointing at him with a fist full of small clothes. "That's what you have. An overactive imagination and an overactive libido." She shoved the garments into her traveling bag. "You probably would've kissed your horse if I hadn't been handy."

Ian crossed the room and twirled her around. Cupping her flushed cheek, he slid his arm around her and pressed her to him. "The only overactive imagination here is yours, little one," he said as his mouth descended on hers.

She trembled, as he tasted the edges of her lips, begging her to open to him. On a sigh, she bade him enter, and into pleasant oblivion he went. She dropped the clothes, letting them fall where they may, and wrapped her arms around his neck as he deepened the kiss.

He'd thought of nothing but kissing her, touching her, feeling her shapely body pressed to his, the torment nearly his undoing. Then with her constant scrutiny, he could take no more. She did not know how her eyes more than studied him, they consumed him, heated his desire for her to near unbearable heights.

Reluctantly, he lifted his head. Her deep brown eyes were open to mere slits and a faint smile played at the corner of her lush mouth.

"Now do you know why I kissed you?" he asked.

She shook her head. "No, and I don't care," she replied breathlessly. "Just kiss me again."

Never one to disappoint a lady, he nibbled at her lips then followed a delicious path along her cheek to her neck. Her long locks fell from the poorly arranged coif and he buried his nose in the mass. The rosewater she'd rinsed her hair with still clung to the tresses and her skin.

"Ian?" she whispered.

"Hmm?" he nibbled along her neck and relished her sigh of pleasure.

"Am I really imagining things?"

He lifted his head and looked at her worried frown. "What do you think you are imagining? My touching you? Tasting you?" he asked with a quick lick at her lips. "The feel of my desire pressing against your soft flesh?"

She shook her head and swallowed deeply. "Am I imagining that there's more to this than just sex?"

Ian sobered rather quickly at that and placed a small bit of space between them as he considered the possibility. Was there more? More than an insatiable desire to bed the woman? One he'd been living with for days upon days?

"The truth please," she said, her eyes no longer heavy with desire. "Not what you think I want to hear."

He searched the depths of her large eyes. The fear of rejection, the insecurity. He had taken this too far.

"I-I'm not saying that we aren't going to—" she stammered. "I mean, I want to, but I just need to know—"

"Hush, sweeting," he said, and pressed a kiss to her brow then cradled her head beneath his chin while holding her tight. He had made love to many women, but he was a gentleman, and he would not trifle with a lady. A virgin, to be precise. And although Jenny Maxwell was from a different time, she was very much a lady. How many times on this insane trip had he reminded himself of that fact? Apparently not enough.

She sighed heavily, warming his chest with her breath. "I ruined it, didn't I?" she asked, her fingers toying with his lacings.

How does one tell a woman that he cannot bed her? He'd never faced such a problem before, having been able to avoid such situations without much difficulty in the past. But thrown together on this journey, he had nearly succumbed to his desires.

"Nay, little one," he said, and stroked her fair cheek, hoping the right words would come to him.

Her sweet lips turned down at the corners. "You know it might help if you'd quit calling me that. In case you've failed to properly ascertain my age, I am twenty-eight years, three months, four days, and..." she glanced at her time piece hidden beneath her sleeve on her wrist. "Eighteen point two hours old. I am not a child." Her lips turned down further as she cocked her head to the side in thought. "Come to think of it, I'm beyond the marrying age for this century, firmly on the shelf, well passed my prime—"

Ian crushed her full lips with his, happily cutting her off in mid-sentence. He did so enjoy interrupting her, it riled her well and true, setting off wondrous sparks in her eyes and brought a flush to her skin. Unfortunately, this new tactic was not helping his current situation.

Moving to her neck, a most delectable spot, he nibbled while he spoke. "I call you little one, not because I think of you as a child, but because you are a dainty, delicate morsel, sweet and soft, and pure. A temptation I find very hard to resist." But resist he would. This is as far as they would go, albeit he would suffer for hours. Nay, days.

"Oh," she sighed, melting against his body. "In that case I won't complain about the nickname anymore. But it isn't very accurate," she said with a soft moan.

"Nay." He moved to her ear and sucked the lobe into his mouth. "You are sweet, I can taste you. And you are soft," he said, gently cupping her breast in one hand while exploring the curve of her hip with the other. "I can feel you."

She moaned and pressed her breast more firmly into his hand. "But I'm not pure."

Ian fell still for a moment then lifted his head. "What did you say?"

She blinked rapidly and opened her mouth several times before she found the words. "I'm—I'm not a virgin. I assume that's what you meant by pure."

His mouth hung agape, while her beautiful face twisted with concern.

"Does it matter that much?" she asked, her brow pinched. "I mean I know that in this century virginity is important, prized, actually, but in mine it's different. Most people, well, not that I do, but others—" She planted her fists on her hips and scowled at him. "I only did it once, okay? I'm in the minority, if you must know. Eighty-eight percent of women my age engage in pre-marital sex and with more than one partner."

She held up her finger and waved it at him. "One, I had one partner and did it one time." She dropped the offending digit and cocked her head to the side. "I realize that it only takes once to lose my virginity, and it wasn't all that great, either," she added under her breath. "But it happened and I can't undo it," she said with a firm nod as she crossed her arms.

Lord, he did so love the way her mind worked. She couldn't stop with a simple yes or no. A full and often detailed explanation burst forth from her regardless of the circumstances.

"Are you laughing at me?" she asked, fury building in her eyes.

"Nay, sweeting," he snatched her up before she fully lost her temper and kissed her.

She pressed her hands to his chest and pulled her lips from his. He clearly saw the questions and confusion burning in her eyes. "I will not lie and say that I am glad of it, but I am relieved in that I would not be the one to take it from you," he said.

"Why not?"

"Although what I want, what we can share, is far more than sex, I am not your husband. I would not take what is rightfully his due."

A small *oh* escaped her lips upon a sigh and the questions were no more. He lifted her and after kicking her bag out of the way, gently placed her on the bed. Stretching out along side her, he ran a finger up the column of her throat to her lips.

"If you wish to cry nay, now is the time. Because I doubt I will be able to stop once we have begun," he said, his voice hoarse with need. By the saints! He had never wanted a woman so much before.

"No more interruptions. This stopping and starting is killing me," she said, and pulled him down for a heady kiss.

This delicate creature, this fey-like woman possessed more passion than he ever imagined. But he should have known. When Jenny approached a task, no matter how large or how small, she gave all of her self to it. Thank the Almighty he was her current mental and physical occupation.

Slowly, he peeled away her clothes, more than pleased to see her perfect form in the dim light of the early evening. Not a scar, not a blemish, not even a birthmark marred her ivory skin. She was perfection in a world where he'd known only imperfection.

"Exquisite," he whispered roughly.

"You can forgo the pretty words, Ian. I don't have to hear them."

He lifted his gaze from the bounty that lay before him and caught sight of the apprehension in her eyes before her lashes swept down to hide it.

Although not a virgin, she had not been loved as a woman aught. He could see that clearly, and wished he could pummel the cur that had made her feel so inferior.

"You are a rare woman, Jenny Maxwell. A rare beauty," he said stroking her cheek. "Ne'er let another soul tell you otherwise."

She lifted her lids with a furrowed brow. "That's a nice thing to say, but—"

"'Tis the truth, sweet Jen. I swear it. I have ne'er lied to you, and I ne'er will." He lowered his lips to hers and began the long slow journey of loving this fragile beauty.

From her welcoming lips he moved down the column of her neck to the sweet peaks of her breasts. Lingering there for a while, relishing her soft moans of pleasure.

Her tiny hands slid beneath his doublet and slipped it from his shoulders. Ian sat up and pulled his shirting over his head and tossed the garments across the room.

"All of it," she whispered, trailing her trembling fingers down his chest.

He swallowed hard at the sensation then forced himself to pull away from the wonderful torment. Stripping out of his breeches, he paused before returning to the bed, letting her eyes have their fill. This was her one last chance to cry off.

She lifted her hand and beckoned to him, her face and body tinted pink with the flush of desire. He could no more refuse her than he could cease the rising of the sun. And he did not wish to.

He returned to her and with kisses, nibbles, and licks he explored her fair skin. Her sighs of contentment spurred him onward as he moved lower and lower to the center of her heat.

Jenny gasped at the touch of his lips against her sex.

"Easy, little one," he whispered, his breath sending a wave of warmth rippling across her skin.

Easy? Hardly! This was an entirely new experience. Her one time didn't consist of a lot of touching and tasting. And Ian seemed intent on his task to examine—no, taste—every inch of her. This was what heaven was like, Jenny thought.

Then she thought again as his deft fingers slid inside her as he tantalized her with his mouth. Her legs drifted further apart as he plucked and sucked. She released the death grip she had on the blanket and spread her hands into the thick crop of fair curls on his head. Urging him on, begging for more, until her body arched against him and a faint but high-pitched cry burst from her throat. Stars darted across the backs of her lids as her lungs begged for oxygen, but she didn't care. She wouldn't mind dying like this, not at all. It was the most extraordinary sensation she'd ever had.

Her tight throat suddenly opened with a sharp inhale, filling her deprived lungs, while her entire body quivered as if she'd run a marathon. She opened her eyes and tried to focus on something, anything, her mind still swirling, then he was there. His piercing blue eyes gazing into hers, he positioned his body above her, supporting his weight upon his elbows, and gently removed her spectacles and set them aside.

"That was..."

"Aye. And 'tis not o'er yet," he said, his voice low and firm.

He slid into her still quivering body, his jaw clenching. Beneath her hands at his back she could feel his muscles tense and ready. Yet he held back, moved slowly and surely, deeper inside her. Her lids grew heavy with the sensual glide of their bodies, building, ever building toward release.

A low growl sounded in his throat as he pressed his mouth to her neck and increased the pace. Faster and faster, deeper and deeper, until she thought she might break apart with the onslaught. And yet she returned every thrust, taking pleasure in his urgency and her own.

A floodtide of sensations swiftly poured over her like liquid mercury, cool and pure, filling every crevice and pore of her body and soul, stealing all thought. No theories, no questions, not even an idle hypothesis was present in her mind. She was filled with nothing but absolute bliss.

At the highest peak of her pleasure, Ian threw back his head, the corded muscles in his neck taut as a hoarse cry erupted from his throat and he pulled out the last second before climaxing.

She bit her lip, hating the sense of loss that snaked through her. It was silly to feel that way, she'd experienced the most intense climax of her life, but his withdrawal reminded her that their situation was temporary, a fling, nothing more. But she could do this, would do this, and damn the consequences.

His forehead came to rest against hers as their pounding hearts slowed and rapid breaths subsided. "You are fey, I have no doubt of it now," he said hoarsely.

She cupped his face in her still shaking hands and kissed him. She would survive, perhaps battered and bruised, maybe even broken in the end, but it was well worth it.

Ian moved to lie beside her, enjoying the feel of her sated body curled against him. He stroked her cheek as her lids drifted shut. "Sleep, little one."

"You'll stay?"

"Aye, to leave you now would be most disagreeable." Odd, though, he'd never done the like before. He always left long before sunrise.

She giggled softly. "You mean you like sleeping in a bed for a change."

"Nay, sweeting. I like sleeping with you, there is a vast difference." Which was the heart of the problem. She was different.

He kissed her soft lips and she smiled then snuggled in tighter against his side. But he could not deny that this was what lovemaking should be like, what he'd imagined it to be like. Although he had thoroughly enjoyed his many liaisons, this was something else, something new, and he liked it. Quite a bit.

But he feared he would soon make a grave mistake. He'd nearly lost his senses with her sweet body beneath him, the feel of her slick pulsing heat, beckoning him to the edge. With the last ounce of his control, he'd pulled himself from her warmth, praying he'd been in time. He would not bring about a bastard like himself, destroying the life of the woman lying contented in his arms. Yet he would enjoy this moment, this night, and any others she cared to share with him, for their time was short. Her life was in the future, where she wished to be, where she belonged.

Pushing the sad thought from his mind, he said, "I will, however, leave you after midnight, sweeting."

"Why?" she asked sleepily.

"Michael is to relieve me of my watch, and 'twould be in poor form to announce our...situation."

She lifted her head and peered at him in the dim firelight, a teasing grin on her lips. "Are you trying to save my reputation?"

"Most definitely."

She giggled and laid her head against his chest. "You really are Prince Charming, even if I'm no Cinderella. But I'd much rather you stay here and keep me warm all night than worry about what others will say. Besides, it wouldn't be logical, we're married," she said with a small yawn. "And Michael's not foolish enough to risk making you angry with any comments."

Ian grinned at her reasoning. "'Tis true Michael will say little, sweeting, but I fear he has already sworn to defend your honor."

"That's sweet," she muttered.

"Aye, sweet," he mumbled, hating what it truly meant. That he would indeed have to leave the comfort of her bed and soon.

He pulled the covers up over her shoulder and pressed a kiss to the crown of her head. For once he did not wish to argue with her, but he would leave at the appropriate time.

Chapter Ten

The next morning their little band was on the road once again. Jenny couldn't stop glaring at Michael's back. If not for him, she would've woken in Ian's arms. He wanted to stay, she knew he did. He'd kissed her before he left, and whispered his regret, thinking she was asleep. She had so wanted to stop time and stay in bed with him forever. The man was amazing, of course her limited experience gave her nothing to compare him to, not really, but wow was no longer enough to describe him.

"'Twould be best if you thought on something else, sweeting, before I find myself looking for a secluded spot where those thoughts might become reality," Ian said with a wink.

She schooled her features and gave him a superior grin. "I've no idea what you're talking about. I was calculating the number of hours it will take to reach Arreyder at this pace."

He chuckled. "In a hurry are we? And what awaits us there? Let me see, a pregnant bossy woman who will demand most of your time. An overbearing Scot who can do nothing but worry and be a nuisance to you and his wife. A doting aunt and soon to be grandfather who will also demand much of your attention with their never-ending questions." He sighed as he shook his head. "Nay, I do not wish to hurry our journey." He cast her a wicked grin, and said, "I wish to have you to myself for as long as may be."

Her heart tipped sideways, and she smiled. "But you don't have me to yourself," she said, nodding toward Michael's back.

"True, not completely. Not yet. But there will be ample opportunities, little one. I promise you," he said, and reached across and brushed her cheek with the back of his fingers.

Warmth enveloped her and she barely refrained from following his hand as he drew it away.

They rode for hours, pausing only long enough for lunch before stopping for the night. It looked like rain, so Ian and Michael tied the meager shelter amid some trees for protection. There would be no loving tonight, she thought as she sat beneath the canopy.

They ate a light dinner and settled down to sleep with her in the middle.

Ian took her hand and pressed a soft kiss to the back. "If you should grow cold, feel free to share my blanket," he whispered, a devilish gleam in his eye.

She lifted her hand and sifted a few stray locks of his hair through her fingers. "I'll keep that in mind."

He sighed and his lids drifted closed. She allowed her hand to travel over his brow, alongside his jaw, and to his lips.

She gasped as he pulled one of her fingers into his mouth and sucked. Mesmerized by the sensation, the subtle grin teasing the corners of his mouth, a low moan threatened to ease out. She bit her lip to keep it at bay and lifted her gaze to his.

He knew what he was doing to her. He knew with every stroke of his tongue, every pull of his mouth, that he stoked a white-hot fire low in her belly. That her breasts tingled and ached for attention, that the apex of her thighs grew moist and ready for him. This was what it was to have a man who knew how to make love to a woman. And he was all hers...for now.

Ian pulled her finger from his mouth and leaned over her, longing for a taste of her. His mouth met hers and he feasted on her sweetness. Damn Michael, he had best be a deep sleeper, for he could not ignore the hunger burning inside him. He had to have her.

She pushed at his chest and he lifted his head, knowing he would be told quite simply to go back to his own pallet. But she surprised him. Deftly, she slid her small hand into his breeches and wrapped her fingers around him. He could not withhold his moan of pleasure. She slapped a hand over his mouth with a silent giggle and eyed their sleeping comrade.

Seeing that Michael still slept, Ian moved his hand

beneath her skirts and found her dewy curls. She tossed her head back, and he quickly covered her mouth with his before a moan or more could escape from her lovely throat.

They made not a sound, not a moan as they pleasured one another, their gazes keenly locked. He watched with utter fascination as she climaxed beneath him, and he quickly followed suit. 'Twas one of the most unusually satisfying experiences of his life.

Their breathing returned to normal and he returned to his pallet. Facing one another on their sides, he found her hand and laced his fingers with hers. He watched her nod off rather quickly, as was her way, but wearing a sweet smile. He couldn't say how long he watched her sleep before fatigue took him as well, but he knew that when he awoke in the morning, her face was what he wanted to see first.

But when morning came, 'twas not Jenny's sweet face he saw, but an empty place where her head had rested. He blinked a moment or two, noted Michael's still sleeping form, then jumped to his feet with a sudden rush of fear.

She was gone.

Heart in his throat, he spun about looking for any sign of her. Their horses were still tethered where they'd left them, and 'twas no sign of a struggle, perhaps—and he prayed it was so—she had merely gone off for some privacy. But he could not stand still and wait for her return. He paced the small clearing, looking for clues to her direction. Finding broken branches amid the brush, he ventured into the wood on stealthy feet.

Humming, sweet and soft, reached his ears and he nearly fell to his knees with thanks. As she tromped toward him through the wood, he leaned against the tree and waited.

"A pleasant morning to you, mistress," he said, as she drew near.

"Oh! Ian, you startled me."

He wanted to rail at her for wandering so far away without protection, but her bright smiling face dulled his annoyance.

She came closer and he pulled her into his arms. "Do

you have any idea what I thought upon waking?"

Her hands linked about his neck and she looked up at him. "Mmm, you thought I'd been snatched by an evil knight and was being held captive in a dark castle high in the mountains."

With a chuckle, he kissed the tip of her nose. "You are full of fantasy this morn, but the tale is not far from the truth."

Her teasing grin fell somewhat. "I'm not in any danger. I've thought about that first day more thoroughly and have concluded that it's highly likely that whoever the man was, he didn't know I was there until I screamed. Why else would he have done nothing while I was stumbling around?"

"Biding his time for the perfect opportunity."

"For what? I'm not worth anything to anyone here. No money, no ransom, there's no logical reason for anyone to want to grab me."

He pressed her closer. "You are wrong, little one. You are a rare find, one any man would be proud to call his. By theft if necessary."

His words seeped into Jenny's soul and took root. Her hands slid behind his neck and she pulled him down for a thorough kiss. Her heart was going to be broken, there was no doubt now. She was in love with Ian Southernland. A man no woman could tame, no woman could keep to herself.

His arms tightened and he moaned low and deep. "God help me. I want you."

"Isn't that a coincidence." Her fingers, not quite as skilled as they were the night before, struggled to release him from his pants. Never did she think she would ever behave this way with a man, so forward, so demanding...so free. Loving Ian with her body and soul did things to her, changed her, and she relished it with a fervor.

"Nay. We cannot," he choked, stilling her hands.

"Oh." She stilled, suddenly cold. "I'm sorry," she said, lowering her eyes and pulling away, "you said you wanted me, so I thought—it doesn't matter what I thought. We should be getting back."

He pulled her against him and tilted her face up. "I

want you more than I have ever wanted a woman in my life. But I will not take you like a rutting stag in the wood." His grim frown eased. "I want to pleasure you in ways you cannot fathom, in a bed of eiderdown and silk sheets for hours—nay, days on end."

"And last night?" she asked, her voice quivering with renewed need.

"Last eve, I lost my head. I am...better today."

She grinned knowingly. "Care to test that theory?"

His eyes widened. "Sweet Jen, do not tempt me, I beg of you."

"Ian," she breathed, and brushed her lips across his. Moving across his strong clenching jaw, she found his ear and circled it with her tongue, bringing a low groan from deep in his chest.

Never having felt this sort of power, she was giddy with it, and nearly laughed aloud. Oh what a delicious turn of events.

"Touch me," she whispered, guiding his strong hand to her breast.

He flattened his back against the tree as she rubbed against his erection. "You are determined to kill me, I fear."

"Just a *little* death."

Fisting his hand in her hair, he tilted her head back and stole her breath with a crushing kiss. Their tongues entangled in a fevered frenzy, neither hearing the crunching of leaves and twigs growing closer.

The game, the power, had turned on her. She wanted him as much if not more than he wanted her, but something made her pause. Ian stilled as well, his breath fast against her cheek.

"'Tis Michael, I wager. Searching for us," he said.

"Why?"

"Your honor, remember?"

With a deep breath, she pulled away and straightened her clothes. "I can't believe I thought it was sweet," she growled.

Ian chuckled and took her hand. The nearly blinding pain beneath his breeches would be evident to the lad, and would likely prove that he had not taken the lady's virtue, but it did not ease him in the least.

They met Michael some yards away, and although he glowered at Ian at first, a twisted grin laced his mouth as they returned to camp.

"I will repay that bloody Scot in the lists," Ian mumbled.

"Can I help?" Jenny whispered.

He kissed her hand with a wide smile. "You can tend his wounds when I am done with him."

"Maybe," she said with a grin.

They gathered their gear and continued on. Deciding it was in his best interests to avoid Innes, they did not sleep at the farmhouse again, but traveled on. If Jenny was indeed jealous, and Innes pursued him with more vigor, he would find himself in a most disagreeable position. 'Twas best to avoid the conflict. And with their early departure from Edinburgh there were many hours of daylight still left of which to travel. There was no need to seek shelter at the farm.

Their second night was spent much the same as the first, but Ian did no more than give Jenny a peck on the lips good night once Michael had turned his back. He held his grin at her charming pout as he turned onto his side facing away from her. Although he had been thoroughly pleased with the previous nights' events, he ached to be inside her after her tormenting him in the woods. The ride had been most uncomfortable all afternoon and plagued him still, but he would refrain. He had to.

****

Waking to a new day and a lingering ache beneath Ian's belt, they made for the boat. He did not relish the short trip across the loch. Although Michael was beginning to become a rather large nuisance, he was glad the man was with them. If his seasickness took a firm hold, he would be of little use in protecting Jenny.

Eyeing the loch as they neared the dock, he breathed a sigh of relief at the calm water. He made the arrangements and within minutes they were on board and on their way home.

"I'll be glad tae see home," Michael said.

"And I can't wait to see Tuck," Jenny said, a bright smile on her face as she looked to the Isle Of Mull. "And everyone else."

"And I cannot wait to have you safe behind the stone walls of Arreyder," Ian murmured, already noticing a keen interest in Jenny by at least one man aboard ship.

She let out a heavy sigh. "Ian. I love to hear all the nice things, the compliments and so forth, but aren't you blowing things out of proportion? I'm just a girl, not much different than any other. No one is out to get me."

She turned and looked across the deck. "Look over there. Do you see her? She's very pretty—well once you get past the dirt on her face. But look at her bone structure, the color of her hair, her figure. If you cleaned her up and put her in a ball gown and glass slippers, she'd be the perfect Cinderella."

"Cinderella?" Michael asked.

"Yes, um, it's a fairytale. A story."

"Tell us of this Cinderella," Ian said, noting the soft flush of pink in her cheeks. He doubted 'twas from the breeze blowing across the bow.

"Well, it's about a girl who is forced into a life of servitude by her stepmother and stepsisters until her fairy godmother dresses her in the finest gown, complete with glass slippers, and sends her to a ball where she meets—um—well...Prince Charming," she said, looking anywhere but into his eyes, "and he falls in love with her and saves her from her evil stepmother," she finished hurriedly.

After her comment in the wood about an evil knight, Ian was beginning to see a side of this woman he would never have believed existed. In her heart she was still a girl with dreams of happy endings. Even with her science and facts, she had not let go of her childlike fantasies.

"Is there no battle in this tale?" Michael asked.

"Sorry, no. There's no battle."

Michael grumbled and walked away as the import of what she had said filtered through Ian's brain. She'd called him Prince Charming the first night they had made love, but said she was no Cinderella. What did that mean? Somehow he felt she was being unkind to herself while donning him with a mantel of perfection, which he was not.

He slipped his arm around her waist as they looked out over the loch and lowered his lips to her ear. "'Tis the same fabled Prince Charming Amelia has named me?" he asked, wanting to be certain of the reference.

"Yes, but you see he's become more of a general term now. More of a standard."

One in which women of her time held the men of their acquaintance to as a guide. And, apparently, he had passed the test.

He kissed her temple, pleased that she would see him in such a light, however misguided. "I am honored that anyone would deem me so gallant. But I disagree with much of what you have said, sweeting."

She lifted her gaze to his. "Oh?"

"I am no Prince Charming and you are not just a girl."

She shook her head. "But—"

"I am a man of honor, but I am not this perfection you have created. I am a man with many faults." He looked to the girl across the deck. "And as for the young woman, I agree that she would be quite fetching with some proper grooming. But there is more to a beautiful woman than simply her appearance. 'Tis in the tilt of her stubborn chin," he said, tweaking hers, "the gleam of intelligence in her large brown eyes." He ran his thumb across her bottom lip. "The seductive pout of her lips when she's disappointed. Many things make a woman beautiful, little one, and you are the most beautiful woman I have ever known."

Her mouth opened and closed several times, her eyes large with astonishment. "That's not possible." She blinked and focused on the lacings of his doublet. "I'm not beautiful, not like that. I'm average, at best. You haven't seen the women in my time."

"I have had the pleasure of meeting two women from your world. Both beautiful, although both very different. You, however, are the more lovely of the two."

She shook her head, a deep crease forming between her brows.

"You cannot sway me in this, little one." He tilted up her chin and kissed her.

"You two are makin' a spectacle of yerselves," Michael grumbled.

Jenny grinned beneath Ian's lips, partially at

Michael's comment, but mostly at the way Ian had described her. Fantasy, all of it. She was his current interest, the girl of the moment, and he'd likely said something similar, if not verbatim, to any number of women, but it was still a joy to hear.

"I think," she said, turning in Ian's arms to look at Michael, "that you're just missing Fiona." The young Scot sighed with a scowl and a nod. "I think too, that when we reach shore that you should get on your horse and hurry on to Arreyder," she added. "Ian can keep me safe for the few hours it takes to get there."

Michael lifted his head and looked at Ian, his face not hiding his hope that he would agree.

She felt Ian's chuckle rumble against her back as his arms slid around her waist. "Aye, lad. Make for home as quick as can be. The lady and I shall be fine."

His smile bright, Michael lowered his gaze to Jenny. "Are you sure you be wantin' this, lass? I'm no' convinced you'll be *safe*," he said, cutting his eyes at Ian.

"Contrary to my size, I'm quite a grown woman who can make up her own mind, Michael. I'll be fine. Trust me. I know what I'm doing."

"Well, if you be sure."

She nodded then the Scot turned and looked eagerly to shore. To home and his love. She envied him, the future he had with Fiona. Although life was hard here, they would be happy together as man and wife.

Jenny wrapped her arms around Ian's at her waist, urging him to hold her tighter, wishing their affair was more than it was, that there was a future for them. But a rogue could not be tamed, at least not by her.

Minutes later Michael jumped to the dock before the boat had settled alongside the roughhewn planks. Jenny and Ian laughed at his eagerness. Once the horses were unloaded, they said goodbye to the young man.

"I just realized something," Jenny said. She turned to look at Ian, his gaze on Michael as he disappeared around the corner of a small building at the edge of town. "You didn't get seasick."

He gave her a lopsided grin. "My thoughts were otherwise occupied, sweeting. And quite happily."

She cleared her throat, oddly nervous to be alone

with him. "Can we look around a bit before we go? It looks to be market day."

"Aye, that it is. But you have naught left to buy. You said as much before we left Edinburgh."

"I can still look can't I?"

He chuckled and took her hand as they lead their horses away from the dock. "Some things even time does not change."

She shot him a look, but had to admit he was right. Men were the hunters and women were the gatherers. So, in a way, the need to shop was genetically passed from mother to daughter.

They tied their horses to a rail and strolled along the waterfront by various vendors. A man, seeing Ian's fine clothes, did his best to convince him that he needed a new cloak and heaven knows what else. While he haggled with the man, Jenny slipped away to look at some bolts of cloth. She wasn't much of a seamstress, but with Elspeth and Fiona's help she thought she might be able to create a few more gowns for herself. After all she couldn't travel home until the next solstice, almost six months away.

"Oh, I'm sorry," she said, bumping into a man standing beside her as she turned. "I didn't see you there." She started to step around him, when he caught her arm.

"Come quietly and no one will get hurt," he hissed in her ear.

Jenny froze as the feel of something familiar poked her ribs. A gun.

She swallowed down her spurt of fear and cast a glance at the hooded man. "I know you," she whispered.

"This way," he said, pulling her away from the cloth vendor.

Her feet followed automatically for several yards as she filtered through the catalog of names and faces in her mind and found him.

"Vernon Cox," she said, and jerked to a halt.

"Doctor Cox," he snarled.

He yanked on her arm, but seeing as he wasn't much larger than she, her feet remained firmly planted. "How did you get here? When did you get here?"

"Same as you."

"You followed me?"

"I said I did, didn't I? Now, come on."

"Why?"

"What do you mean, why? Because I'm the one with the gun."

She eyed his weapon, the barrel still pressed to her side, then eyed the man. "I don't think you'll shoot me. What purpose would it serve? Especially since you seem so intent on taking me somewhere."

His jaw clenched beneath a patchy beard. "Fine. I won't shoot you, but I'll shoot him," he said, nodding in Ian's direction, his back to them.

All the blood rushed to her feet and she forced herself not to sway. "No, you wouldn't."

Ian turned, obviously looking for her. The moment his gaze found her, his hand fell to the hilt of his sword and his body stiffened.

Jenny prayed. "I'll go with you," she said, and practically dragged Vernon away.

"I thought as much," the little man said with a sneer.

But Jenny could hear Ian's feet pounding against the earth, rapidly catching up with them. She had to do something! Oh, if only she had her purse and all those rolls of pennies!

Vernon cast a harried glance over his shoulder and pulled the gun from her ribs and aimed it at Ian.

"No!" She twisted and grabbed his arm, bringing the gun down just as it went off.

The impact, sharp and hot, brought Jenny to the ground. Vernon cursed and kicked dirt into her face as he ran away. She recognized it as the same voice she'd heard in the woods a week before, but her thoughts were more in tune with the searing heat scorching the side of her leg and the fierce howl of another man.

Ian.

Chapter Eleven

The blast, a nearly deafening sound, sent a wave of such dread through Ian's body he stumbled as he ran toward Jenny now lying on the ground. He caught sight of the man as he disappeared into the milling crowd, but as much as he wanted to chase after the whoreson who had done this, there was no one he could trust to care for Jenny. All he knew was a staggering pain in his chest at the sight of blood on her dress. He fell to his knees beside her.

Cupping Jenny's sweet face, his voice tight with fear, he called her name. "Jenny! Can you hear me, love?"

Her brow furrowed, she lifted her lids. Pain reflected in the deep brown depths. "I'm alright. I think."

He looked down along her body at the blood seeping through her dress at her thigh.

Her voice was shaky and weak, she said, "I'll—" she swallowed hard and took a deep breath. "I'll need some privacy to examine the wound. I think the bullet went all the way through, but I can't be sure."

"Aye." With trembling arms, he lifted her and turned toward the nearest house. A woman standing in the doorway waved him in, her brow creased with concern.

Amelia had described the advances made to firearms in her time, but he'd never dreamt he would be witness to the horrific effects. And not on a woman. His woman.

He gently placed her in a chair by the fire. "Do you have a bit of cloth for binding?" he asked the old lady.

"No," Jenny said, her voice firmer than before. "Thank you, but I'll use part of my shift."

Ian nodded, agreeing that her shift would likely be cleaner than what the woman could provide. He pulled his dagger from his belt and started to lift her dress then paused, casting a glare over his shoulder at the people gathered in the doorway.

"Be gone with ye," the old woman snapped and shut the door in their faces.

Satisfied they had at least some bit of privacy, he lifted Jenny's dress and looked to her wound. Her lily-white legs, soft and supple and perfect would now hold a scar. The whoreson would pay most dearly for this.

"It doesn't look too bad," Jenny said, her breathing short and quick. "Is there an exit wound?"

He peered beneath her thigh then let out a sigh of relief. "Aye. Now sit back before you faint. I shall bind this for now, then we shall return to Arreyder where Amelia can tend you."

She did as he asked and sat back, but argued with him. What more could he expect? "I'm not going to faint, and Tuck shouldn't be the one to take care of this. Too stressful in her condition. I can manage—"

"Be still, woman," he growled. Her prattle was a good sign, but he was not up to a lengthy discussion. His hands shook as he cut away part of her shift and bound her leg.

"Here lass," the old woman said, shoving a cup under Jenny's nose. "'Tis but a wee dram of whiskey."

"No, thank you. I'm fine."

Ian snapped his head up. "Drink it. Now."

She scowled at him, but did as he commanded with a short cough and gasp. He finished his task and lowered her skirts.

"Yer horses are just outside," the old woman said. "I had a lad fetch them fer ye."

"Thank you, mistress. We are in your debt," he said, and placed some coins in her dirt smudged hand.

"'Twas nothin'," she muttered, and opened the door.

Ian scooped Jenny into his arms as carefully as he could so as not to harm her, but her hiss of pain was evident. "I'm sorry, little one."

"Not your fault," she growled, and let out a long breath as they neared their mounts. "It's Vernon's, that snake."

He paused by her horse, his mind spinning. "You know the man who did this?"

"Afraid so. He was the man that first day in the woods. And Ian. He's not from around here, if you catch my drift."

He carefully placed her on his horse, the weight of her words heavy on his mind. He had known the weapon was not of his time, the gun was nothing he had ever seen before, but the man wielding it?

"We shall discuss this along the way," he said, and sat behind her and slipped his arm around her waist.

Leading Jenny's horse behind them, Ian made his way out of the small village toward Arreyder, his eyes scanning for any sign of the man called Vernon.

"Tell me what you know of him," he demanded.

With a sigh, she leaned into him, her head resting on his shoulder. "His name is Vernon Cox. He's a scientist. My father and he made some deal and I was set to work on Vernon's latest discovery, EQ13. It was a success, of a sort."

"What is this EQ13?"

"It's a drug that reduces dietary fat absorption. Plainly put, it's a diet pill. It doesn't work much better than any others already on the market, but it does work."

"If this EQ13 is a success, then why would he wish to harm you?"

"I don't know. I'll ask him next time I see him," she said wearily.

"Not if I have aught to say about it," he growled.

"It's only logical. He wants me for something. Why else try and kidnap me?"

"Aye, why indeed?" He kissed her forehead. "Rest now," he said, but she was already asleep. The shock, the loss of blood, and the whiskey had taken their toll.

An hour later he eased up the edge of Jenny's dress and looked at the bandages. The bleeding appeared to have slowed, but he knew that infection could set in. She was not out of danger yet. He prayed Amelia had medicines from the future to tend her properly.

She moaned in her sleep. He knew from experience that a steady ache was setting in. 'Twas not much different than a sword wound, he'd wager. His jaw clenched at the memory of Amelia pouring whiskey into the gash in his shoulder a year ago.

"No," he whispered harshly. He could not allow her to do so to Jenny's leg. There had to be a better way, a way without pain, for he would feel it as keenly as she.

Evening fell as he entered the bailey at Arreyder Castle. "Fetch Colin! Quickly!"

William, one of the Laird's old trusted guards frowned deeply as he waved one of the young lads to do his bidding. "What has happened, lad?" The older man's eyes widened at the sight of blood on Jenny's dress.

"She was wounded by the son of the devil," Ian snarled.

William carefully took her as Ian lowered her into his hands so he could dismount without jarring her overmuch.

Jenny groaned pitifully and lifted her head. "Ian?"

"Here, little one," he said, and took her from William's arms.

William followed him into the main hall. "Did ye kill him?"

"Nay. I dare not chase after him without anyone to guard her."

"I see. After ye get the lass tended tae, meet me in the solar. The Laird will wish tae hear of this."

He'd almost made it to Jenny's chamber when Elspeth and a waddling Tuck, moving with greater speed than he'd have thought her possible, came from the other end of the hall, Colin just behind.

"What's happened?" Amelia demanded.

"She was shot," he said, and shouldered his way into her room, the door screeching on its hinges.

Amelia cursed foully and he quite agreed.

"Colin, fetch my bag. You know the one," Amelia said, and followed him into the room.

Ian laid Jenny on the bed. "Easy, love," he said, as she hissed with renewed pain.

He started to lift her skirts when Elspeth burst into the room. "Out with you, lad. We'll take care of the lass."

"Like bloody hell I will," he growled, and continued with his chore. The bleeding had started again with the handling of her from man to man.

Amelia placed her hand on Ian's as he struggled to undo the bandage with his trembling fingers. "I know what to do, Ian."

"Nay," he choked out. "I shall not let you cleanse the wound as you did mine." His vision blurred, tears, he guessed, brought on by fatigue.

But the truth came clear as he blinked them away. 'Twas the gut wrenching fear of losing Jenny that caused them.

A hand, tiny and pale, touched his arm. Ian lifted his head and found Jenny's deep brown eyes looking up at him.

God help him. He loved her.

Her brow furrowed as she studied him. Did she see his true feelings? Were they written across his face, in his eyes? Did she know his heart was breaking because he could never claim her as his own?

Something powerful hung in the air, Jenny sensed it, could almost see it. She knew Ian was upset because he'd failed to protect her, but it wasn't his fault. How could he, how could any of them have known this would happen?

Guilt and pain flashed across his face. She couldn't bare it. She had to ease his mind somehow. "Ian, you've done enough. Now let Tuck and me take it from here."

"Here, love," Colin panted, as he placed the bag on the bed.

"Thanks," Tuck murmured as she ripped open the med kit. "Ian, I really need you to move."

He took Jenny's hand from his arm and brought it to his lips, his lids clamped closed.

"Colin?" Tuck motioned with her head toward Ian.

"Come, my friend," he said, placing his hand on Ian's shoulder. "The women ken what they're about."

Ian opened his eyes and moved to the head of the bed, Jenny's hand still firmly in his. "Nay, I will stay."

Jenny swallowed the lump in her throat. It was more than guilt. He cared. The rake, the rogue, truly cared about her.

"Fine," Tuck sighed, swiping her brow with the back of her hand.

Jenny jerked her gaze from Ian's, instantly realizing this was far too much stress for her pregnant friend. The last thing she or any of them needed right now was for Tuck to go into labor. "Get her a chair, quickly!"

One appeared and Tuck didn't utter a word as Colin forced her to sit.

"Good, now Elspeth, in that bag there's a bottle of

saline solution," Jenny said. "Open a packet of gauze and douse it then use that to clean the area around the wound after Tuck gets the bandages off."

"I know what I'm doing here, Jen," Tuck grumbled, peeling away the bandage. "So does Elspeth. I've taught her what I could since I wasn't sure you'd be here for the delivery." She lifted her head from her task and grinned. "So shut up and let me work, Doc."

Jenny chuckled roughly. "Sorry. Doctors do make the worst patients."

Tuck looked back to her task. "Not bad. What did he use?"

"You expect me to know?" Jenny hissed as the last of the bandage was removed. "Small gun, short barrel."

"Looks like a .32 or maybe a .38. Hole's too small to be anything bigger. Clean too," Tuck continued as she worked. "Right through the fleshy part of the thigh. You were lucky."

"That's a matter of opinion," she grumbled, examining the hole for herself. She absently noticed Ian's hand still wrapped around hers, but she wasn't letting go. Her stomach was doing funny flips as she examined the injury. That was her leg, her blood. She sucked in a quivering breath and sat back, focusing on the canopy above the bed. Blood loss, whiskey on an empty stomach, fear for Ian's life, it was all catching up with her.

"You want a local or grin and bear it while I clean this?" Tuck asked.

Her gaze lowered to Tuck, her head bent over her task. "I'd rather save the local for something more serious."

That brought Tuck's head up. "I doubt I'll need it, Jen. You know I have an extremely high tolerance for pain."

"I'm the doctor here and I say what I need. And what you may or may not need. Save the anesthetic."

Tuck looked to Ian still standing by the head of the bed, and their clasped hands. "You heard her, so don't get mad at me. But it won't be as bad as whiskey, I promise." Tuck's gaze shifted to Jenny's. "Keep holding onto him, cause even though it won't be as bad, it's still going to hurt like hell."

Jenny nodded.

The moment Tuck began, Jenny squeezed her eyes closed on a hiss and gripped Ian's hand as hard as she could. Dots formed behind her lids.

Ian knelt beside the bed and turned Jenny's face to his. He hurt like the devil himself had sent a spear straight through his heart. Aye, this Vernon Cox was a walking dead man.

"Tell me of the whoreson who did this," he said roughly. "What does he look like?" He needed information to find and kill the fiend, but Jenny also needed a diversion.

She opened her eyes and blinked several times. "He—he—"

Ian nodded, urging her to continue, to keep her mind occupied. "He is a small man, but he wore a hood. I did not see his face."

She took a deep breath and nodded. "He's approximately five foot six," she swallowed hard, "one hundred and forty pounds. Pale skin, brown hair, roughly two inches in length, and—a—patchy—beard." Her voice faded to a squeak in the end and tears filled her eyes and her brow dotted with perspiration.

He jerked his head to the side. "Damn, you Amelia, be quick about it!"

"I'm going as fast as I can," Amelia grumbled.

Ian turned back to Jenny and pressed his face close to hers, their hands locked between them. "'Tis almost over," he said softly, and kissed her whitened knuckles.

Her head began to shake, her lips quivering with what he could only deem as the need to scream, but she held it in. This was no frail female. He had been sorely mistaken in ever thinking such a thing.

"Tell me—tell me how the combustion engine functions," Ian said, grasping at anything to occupy her mind. And his.

Two tears slipped from her eyes and rolled down her cheeks. He brushed one away from the edge of her mouth with the tip of his thumb.

"And these things called airplanes. Tell me how such a thing is capable of leaving the ground. Does it flap a pair of mighty mechanical wings? Or mayhap birds strapped to its belly give it flight." All of which was utter nonsense, but he was at a loss as to how to distract her.

Tight creases formed at the corners of her mouth as a short pain filled chuckle escaped her lips.

"Nay?" he said with a forced smile, his eyes filling as he looked into hers. 'Twould not do to weep before her, his heart would surely be known.

She lifted her trembling hand and stroked his cheek. "Thank you."

He blinked away his pain, his throat tight, and said, "Anything for a lady." How he ached to kiss her, to crawl into the bed alongside her and hold her in his arms, keeping her safe and warm. But he had failed to keep her safe. The guilt would stay with him for the rest of his days.

"The worst is over, Jen," Amelia said.

Elspeth took the bloody gauze from Amelia's fingers as she finished her work. His stomach roiled at the sight. Although never a man to be sick from such a thing, knowing it was his sweet Jen's blood made him ill.

Swallowing the bile rising in his throat, he asked, "Will you have to stitch the wound?" He prayed she would not, for that was more painful than the cleansing.

Tuck shook her head. "No, not a gunshot wound. It's best to keep it bandaged so air can get to it. She's going to ache for a couple of weeks, but she'll be back on her feet before then. Knowing Jenny, we'll have to fight to keep her in bed," she said with a chuckle.

"Like someone else I know," Jenny said, the strength in her voice returning. The news eased some of the tension from Ian's shoulders, but his heart would not recover so quickly.

"Ian," Colin said, pulling his gaze from the women as they wrapped Jenny's lovely leg, now clear of any evidence that she'd been hurt, save for the bandage. "We've a need tae speak."

"Aye," he said with a weighty sigh. He pressed a kiss to Jenny's hand and relished the sweet smile she bestowed on him. One that did not last for long.

"Don't you dare go looking for Vernon," she said, her voice holding no evidence of her previous pain.

Ian paused in the doorway. "You, my dear lady,

concentrate on getting well. I shall do what must be done."

"Colin, don't let him do it! And don't you go after him either. Tuck, tell them," she demanded.

Ian cast a glance at Amelia, her mouth puckered and one brow arched. "You'd better not go anywhere." She shot him a look. "Not until we've talked."

"Dammit, Tuck! Colin, she needs to be in bed. This stress—"

"You calm down or I'll put you out," Amelia said, pointing her finger at Jenny. "Elspeth, I'm counting on you to keep her in bed." She turned to Ian and Colin. "And you two wait for me or I'll follow your butts through the main gates."

Colin growled low. "Doona order me about, woman. You should be abed, as the lass says."

He crossed the room in two strides and scooped Amelia up. Ian cleared the chuckle from his throat at Amelia's response, not something a lady would utter.

"Meet me in the solar," Colin said as he marched past Ian.

He nodded and cast one last glance at Jenny. "All will be well, little one. Rest."

"Ian," she called after him, but his step never wavered.

The stranger wanted to take her away or harm her more severely. Ian could not let him succeed. 'Twould be hard enough on his weary soul when Jenny chose to return home of her own accord. He refused to let anyone interfere with the little time they had together. But more importantly, the vermin had brought Jenny great pain, had scarred her fair skin. Vernon Cox would pay.

Colin joined him in the solar with William and his father in a matter of moments. Colin's gaze darted to his father, a subtle reminder that they must watch their words, as the Laird and William knew nothing of the time portal. Only Elspeth, outside of the four of them knew of its existence.

Laird MacLean lifted his head from the perusal of the flames, his features sour. "Tell me what happened. From the beginning, lad," he demanded.

Ian told of the events, including the man's first

attempts to grab Jenny, and how she suspected his presence had to do with her father.

"We should send word tae the lass's sire," the Laird said.

Colin and Ian exchanged uneasy glances. Ian considered attempting to explain Maxwell's disinterest in his daughter, but thought better of it. "I shall see to it," Ian said.

"William, double the guards at the gate. Colin, lad, I know ye be wantin' tae stay with yer wife, but yer trackin' skills are needed." The old man motioned toward Ian. "You and Colin search the isle for the coward. I'll no' have another person harmed on MacLean soil."

"On the morrow, Da," Colin said with a firm nod. "He is likely on foot and will be some time afore he arrives. I doona wish tae track him from Tobor Morar."

"Aye," Ian said, his head aching. He wanted to find the bloody sod and rip him apart, but knew Colin was correct. They had a much better chance of catching the cur closer to the castle than half way across the island. And God forbid, they should miss him in passing, leaving Jenny vulnerable.

William and Laird MacLean left the solar. William to tend to the night guards, and the Laird to his bed.

Colin placed a hand on Ian's shoulder. "She will be safe, my friend. Trust me," he said, leading Ian down the hall. "Now go rest, for we have much tae do in the morn. There is a rat to be caught and severely dealt with," he said, his mouth turned up in an evil smile.

Ian nodded wearily. His body, his mind, his very soul ached with the impotence of failure. Paying no heed to his direction, he found himself standing at the foot of Jenny's bed watching her sleep. He would not fail her again.

The need to feel her soft form pressed to his, safe and warm, overpowered him. With the silence of a cat, he stripped away his clothes then slid beneath the covers to lie by her side. He wrapped his arm around her waist and pressed his face against her neck, her silky hair his pillow, her sweet scent his breath.

"Your feet are cold," she murmured.

He grinned and pressed a kiss to her shoulder where her night rail gaped exposing her fair skin. "Forgive me," he whispered. "I did not mean to wake you."

"I'm glad you came. I was worried about you." She stifled a yawn.

He held in his chuckle. "Were you now?" It warmed his heart that she cared for him, wanted his presence.

"I thought you'd go chasing after Vernon in the dark. We don't know what other weapons he may have brought with him."

"I shall deal with him soon enough. But I doubt he has naught but the one firearm."

She rubbed her cheek against his head. "A good bit of deduction or a wild guess?"

"Deduction, and you well know it." He lifted his head and peered into her sleepy eyes lit by the flickering firelight. "He would have thought you to be but one small woman who would cause him little trouble," he said, brushing a long strand of hair from her cheek, all the more amazed by her beauty.

Smiling, she said, "He doesn't know me very well, does he?"

"Nay, he does not." He brushed his lips across hers, holding himself back. She was injured and fatigued. He could not make love to her as he wished, but he would hold her for as long as he could. "Now sleep."

"You're going to leave before morning, aren't you?"

He pressed a kiss to her frown. "Aye. You are a lady and I will not harm you unnecessarily."

She sighed and let her lids drift closed as he stroked her cheek. "I'll take what I can get then, and quit complaining. Even if you do have cold feet."

He smiled at her sleepy comment and in but a few breaths she was asleep.

"Pleasant dreams, my love," he whispered, and nestled in beside her, content with her in his arms.

If only their time was not so short. Naught but a handful of months remained before she would take her leave of him. He prayed selfishly that she would stay, although he knew 'twould ne'er be. This was not her time, and he knew that although she enjoyed the sights, the experience, she would not wish to stay.

Chapter Twelve

The following morning, Colin and Ian gathered in the main hall with a full garrison at the ready. Small units were to take turns searching MacLean land. Ian led one group while Colin went in another direction with the second. Neither man wished to venture too far from the castle and the women, fearing for their safety, but they had little choice if they wished to catch the fiend. But a week of searching passed with no results.

Colin and Ian met in the solar, their failure heavy on their shoulders.

"'Tis as if the maggot has vanished," Colin grumbled as he paced before the fire.

"He could've left the island," the Laird said.

Ian shook his head. "Nay, not without Jenny. He has a need of her."

"Ah yes, the lass. 'Tis a pity we know no' what the man wants with her."

"Aye, Da. But Jenny doesna ken his reasoning," Colin said.

"And if Jenny cannot fathom his motives, we shall surely have no luck in divining the answer either," Ian said with a weighty sigh.

Fiona appeared. "Master Southernland, Tuck wishes tae see ye," she said, then dashed from the room. Her pending marriage to Michael but a month away had her flitting about the castle like a drunken butterfly.

"Now, I wonder what my wife would be wantin' with you," Colin said, stroking his chin, a taunting grin on his face.

Ian ignored him as he left the solar, not missing the Scot's chuckle. Although he'd managed to leave Jenny's bed before sunup each morn, he felt certain all in sundry knew where he'd been spending his nights. Although they'd only shared some heated kisses and a small bit of touching, he relished holding her while she slept. 'Twas a small bit of comfort for his weary soul.

He made his way to Amelia's chamber, knowing he was about to be sorely interrogated.

"You wished to see me, dear heart?" he asked, strolling into her chamber as if there was naught wrong with the world. Or his heart.

"Tell me what's going on with you and Jenny," she demanded.

"Nothing of any concern."

"You don't lie and you really suck at evasion, Ian. Spit it out, or you'll be the first to get diaper duty."

He chuckled and took her hand. "You are a treasure, my sweet. But I shall not burden you with my troubles."

"Don't make me hurt you."

He laughed, knowing full well there was sincerity at the heart of her threat. She would make him pay later after the babes had come, of that he had no doubt.

"Look, I've got no problem with you two hanging out," she said. "But I have a feeling there's more going on. And it's not all good."

"Aye," he admitted, his heart heavy. "I seem to have an uncanny knack for choosing the wrong women to care for. Present company excluded."

"Why is she the wrong woman? Can't you handle her having all those brains?"

"Nay! I rather like the way she thinks." And how he managed to win many an argument by kissing her. "'Twould be a dreadful bore to have a woman that possessed no sense," he said, reining in his thoughts.

"Then what's the problem?"

With a sigh, he raked his fingers through his hair and paced to the window. He may as well tell her, she was his friend and perhaps she could soothe his heart somewhat, although he feared 'twas a lost cause. "She knows not of my status."

"You're gonna have to throw me a rope, here Ian. I'm not following."

He took a steadying breath, and turned to face her. "Do you know why I chose to ride with Colin for so many years, ne'er choosing a wife?"

She shook her head, her brow furrowed beneath her

red curls.

"My mother was a lady of noble birth. She trusted my father, believed his words when he told her he loved her and would marry her. She was heartbroken when he did not." 'Twas why he ne'er lied, for a single falsehood could steal the very life from a person.

He turned back to the window and stared out at the dreary day, feeling it deep in his soul. "A weary sadness was forever in her eyes," he said softly. He blinked away the unhappy memory. "My mother's family had turned her out long before. So when she died my father felt obligated to recognize me as there was no one to take me in." He sniffed. "Recognized, as if that made a difference."

He glanced at Amelia then back to the window, not wanting to see the pity in her eyes. "I have no prospects, no title, and am a bastard son of a baron. No woman of any rank—no lady of gentle breeding will have me as her husband. 'Tis why I am certain Jenny will ne'er see me as anything more than what I am. A temporary diversion in her life. And I, for one, cannot blame her."

A sharp painful tugging of his ear had him bellowing. "Ow! What in bloody hell—" he twisted from Amelia's grasp.

"Ian Southernland, if I wasn't carrying this baby baggage I'd lay you out flat!" She stood, her hands fisted at her wide waist, her green eyes blazing. "Of all the stupidest men...I thought Colin had his moments, but this one!" She paced before him spouting various vile things about men in general, but mostly about him.

"What goes on here?" Colin burst into the room, his face contorted with concern.

Amelia glared at Ian, then turned a sweet smile to her husband. "Nothing, we were talking. And..." she said, getting back in bed, "I'm not going to get up again. I promise. Now scram."

Colin looked at him then at Amelia lying prone in the bed. His mouth poised for comment, Amelia cut him off.

"I'm fine. Honest. But I'm not done with him," she said, shooting Ian a glare.

With a stern frown, Colin stomped from the room.

Ian rubbed his ear as he eased toward the door.

"You take one more step and so help me, I'll knock

you on your ass so fast..."

He stopped in his tracks. "Amelia, dearest, you really should rest and I am doing naught but upsetting you, 'tis obvious."

"Oh, you don't know upset, buddy. Now sit." He eyed the door, curious if he'd make it out of the room before...

"Sit!"

He cringed then returned to his chair. It was best to placate her now and do whatever necessary to keep her and the babes safe.

"First, whether you like it or not—and with your inflated male ego, you'll probably hate this—but Jenny is loaded. We're talking owning small countries, Ian. Not just some estate deal. Get me? So your lack of prospects doesn't mean squat to her."

His jaw fell slack. She had never quite explained Jenny's situation in such a way before. He knew her to be wealthy, but this was more than overwhelming. And nay, he did not like it! It was a man's duty to provide for his wife, not the other way around.

"And as for titles, they don't carry any weight with Jen. Lastly, and I so can't believe you think so little of yourself, but Jenny wouldn't care if you were the result of an alien abduction, much less illegitimate."

"Alien ab—?" She raised her finger, and he instantly closed his mouth.

"That leaves you with two real problems."

"It does?" he asked, trying to grasp it all.

"The time thing bites. She's okay here, but it's not her thing, get me?"

"Um, I am trying, dear heart."

She huffed, and said, "She isn't as comfortable in this time as I am. It's hard on her. She really likes her gizmos and gadgets—you know, her lab equipment and junk."

"Ah, yes, things such as her spectacles."

"Exactly. That and loads of other stuff."

"You mentioned two problems," he said, nearly terrified of the second. The first was naught but a simple thing. He would enjoy seeing her time. Perhaps even live there.

"Jenny probably figures she has to play this thing light because another girl will catch your eye and she'll be old news."

He jumped to his feet. "I may look like my father, I may have his damnable blood running through my veins, but I am not him!"

Amelia smiled. "I never thought it for a minute, but it's good to hear you're a faithful rogue, just the same. So, now that you know what you're dealing with, how are you going to play it?"

"Are you quite certain that she will," he swallowed his trepidation, "welcome my suit?" The thought of Jenny's rejection was beyond terrifying.

"Positive. I think she's falling for you. After all, you're her Prince Charming," she said with a grin. "But remember, I *will* break every bone in your body if you hurt her."

He chuckled and leaned down to kiss Amelia's brow. "I will not trifle with her heart, sweeting. I vow it. For I fear mine is quite involved."

Moments later he knocked upon Jenny's door. She bade him enter and he found her sitting by the fire.

"You should not be out of bed," he said, striding toward her.

"I can't lie there any more. It's boring."

A grin stole over his lips as he scooped her up. "I can think of a few things that may occupy your mind, little one."

She giggled and did not complain or fuss as he carried her to the bed.

He pulled the covers up to her neck and brushed his thumb across her pouty lips. "You sorely tempt me, mistress."

"I thought that was the idea?"

He chuckled. "You are injured. And what I wish to do would not be helpful."

"I'm much better, I've been telling you that for days. I think it would be greatly beneficial," she said lowly, one small hand sneaking out from beneath the coverings to glide up his arm. "I'm the doctor, aren't I? I should know what's best for me." She gripped his doublet and pulled him down for a kiss.

He moaned at the feel of her moist full lips. "I suppose if the physician has prescribed it, who am I to argue?"

She loosened the lacings of his doublet and shoved the clothing aside. He could feel her short nails raking across his fevered flesh over his shirt. In moments he was beneath the covers, feeling her bare skin against his. There would be time later to explore her feelings for him, to see if she would indeed welcome his suit. She would not return to her world for months yet, allowing him the opportunity to fully win her heart. And perhaps her hand in marriage.

Aye, they had all the time in the world.

****

If she didn't get this Gummy Bear recipe right and soon, she'd scream or...throw-up. The smell of the gelatin during processing was nauseating beyond belief. Odd, Jenny thought. Smells hadn't ever been much of a problem for her. Working in a lab and her learning experiences in med-school had numbed her olfactory nerves, psychologically, at any rate.

It had been weeks since she and Ian had returned from Edinburgh and she'd barely made any progress on the recipe. And she really needed to get it right. Tuck was handling her confinement as well as could be expected, but the candy would certainly improve her disposition.

"There you are, dear," Elspeth said as she bustled into the kitchen and over to Jenny's makeshift laboratory. "Michael and Fiona have returned from Tobor Morar with some cloth for your new dresses. When you get time, come tae the solar and we'll have a look at the lot."

"Thank you, Elspeth. I won't be much longer."

"Here ya are, lass," cook said as she placed the latest batch of gelatin on the table then went back to her other chores.

Jenny swallowed hard and pressed a hand to her stomach.

"Why you're as green as can be," Elspeth said. "You look like Amelia, the poor wee thing, during her first months."

The blood drained from Jenny's face to her toes, she knew it had, because she felt certain she was about to faint.

"Jenny, lass, are you no' well?"

She clutched the side of the table and forced herself to breathe. "I'm fine," she squeaked then cleared her throat. "Just a little tired."

"Perhaps you'd best rest. You've been workin' on this concoction for an age. We can look at the cloth later."

"Yes. Yes, that's a good idea. Thank you, Elspeth."

Elspeth left the kitchen with a worried frown.

Her face turned away from the gelatin, Jenny took several deep breaths. How could she have missed it? Her breasts were fuller and more sensitive, smells that never bothered her before bothered her now, she felt *off* in the mornings, and more tired than usual. God, she'd just thought it was time for her period, but as she quickly calculated, she realized she was late. Very late.

"How could I have been so stupid?" she whispered. She wanted to cry, scream...and smile at the same time. She was going to have a baby. Ian's baby. How was she ever going to tell him? And how was she going to tell her father?

Absently, she completed the last steps of her experiment and failed. Not surprising since her mind swirled with the concept of becoming a mother. She would be five months along when it was time to go home. She didn't think that traveling through the portal would harm the fetus, but she was a bit concerned.

Staying, however, was out of the question, she reasoned as she made her way to her room for a nap. She was the only true physician here, and she wouldn't risk the baby's life by giving birth to him under such harsh conditions. She was not Amelia Tucker MacLean.

Considering the similarities between Jenny and her own mother in size and health, and the fact that she had died due to complications during childbirth, could not be ignored. No, she had to have the best care possible and that could only be found in the future.

She laid her head on her pillow and drifted off, forcing her thoughts to settle. It wasn't long before she felt Ian lay down beside her.

"Are you not well, sweeting?" he asked, his lips brushing her brow.

"Just tired. Too much time in the kitchen," she lied. She wasn't ready to tell him about the baby, but she wouldn't be able to keep it a secret for too much longer.

"I didn't expect you back from your search so soon," she said with a yawn. He and Colin went out every day to look for Vernon, but after weeks of searching, he was nowhere to be found. She wondered if he was still alive.

"There is naught a trail to follow. 'Tis a waste of time and effort at this point to continue."

She grinned as he curled her in against his side. "So you've decided to guard me in case he shows up, is that it?"

He chuckled softly. "Aye, you have the right of it. Now rest, love."

****

Vernon shivered with disgust. How long did these McKenzies plan on keeping him here? What had it been three weeks, four? He didn't know any longer. If only he had his gun.

He idly wondered how that brat, Jenny, managed with a bullet in her leg. At least that's where he thought he shot her, the stupid woman. She'd better still be alive, he needed her. But if she wasn't, he could always use that Englishman to get home. He knew how the portal worked.

If he'd had more bullets he would've shot the stupid Scots who'd grabbed him. How the hell was he supposed to know he was on MacKenzie land? It wasn't like there was a sign posted somewhere.

A guard appeared with his lunch. Vernon tried again to convince him that he wasn't a threat, but the man ignored him. He tried to think of a bribe, anything, but he had nothing on him but his borrowed clothes. Except...

"Tell your Laird, that if he wants more firearms like mine, I know where he can get them," Vernon said, grinning at his brilliancy.

Turning his back on the guard, he kicked a rat out of the way and took the wooden bowl from the floor. The first few days, he'd let the rats have it, but the longer they kept him in this dungeon, the more he realized he'd have to eat to keep up his strength.

He'd trick these stupid Scots into thinking he'd lead them to more guns, then he'd make a break for it. Then he'd find Jenny and make her pay for this. It was all her fault. And her father's.

Rogue's Challenge

Chapter Thirteen

Ian had tried to work up the courage to ask Jenny to be his wife, but each time he began, he nearly choked on the words. Not that he didn't wish to wed, quite the contrary. But the thought of her refusing him scared the wits out of him. Their nights together were like nothing he'd ever experienced before. If she refused him, their time together would come to an abrupt end.

He found her in the kitchen yet again fussing with her strange concoctions. Only Tuck knew what she was brewing, or attempting to brew. Something edible he was certain, as he'd seen Jenny taste the odd bit of glop herself. He shivered at the memory. A less palatable creation he had ne'er seen before.

Jenny lifted her latest attempts to her lips. She cocked her head as she tasted the morsel, discerning the various flavors and texture, no doubt.

"I take it from that small grin on your lovely mouth that you have finally succeeded," he said, taking a seat beside her.

"Mmm, as close as I'll get, I think."

"Now may I know what it is? I sorely dislike secrets and this one has nagged at me from the beginning."

"Here," she said, holding out a small unsavory looking glob.

"Must I?"

"You must," she said with a delightful giggle.

He studied the thing in her hand then lifted his gaze to hers. "I would rather spend a day in the lists after Colin has been tossed by Amelia. But for you, sweeting, anything."

Her eyes seemed overly bright as he popped the oddity into his mouth. But before he could contemplate why she seemed overly emotional by his declaration, the sweetness of a ripe strawberry bathed his tongue then melted in glorious bliss.

Jenny blinked away her burgeoning tears and watched Ian's eyes widen as the gummy creation dissolved in his mouth. He couldn't know how his words touched her. If only *anything* was possible.

"Is it acceptable?" she asked, knowing full well it was. She'd gotten the recipe almost perfect, although Maggie had been quite put out by her constant presence in the kitchen. It was well worth the effort. And even though the smells were nearly unbearable, it was something to occupy her mind. It was that or go mad pacing in her room, or examining Tuck far too often. She didn't need her friend suspecting something was wrong. But they would all know eventually.

Ian swallowed and reached for another one. "What do you call it?"

She let him take a few more then shifted the tray away. "At home they're called Gummy Bears, but since I can't make them into small bear shapes, I think they need a new name."

"Mm, a different flavor this time. Tell me how you created this wonder," he said, popping another into his mouth.

He made her smile, something he was always able to do no matter what troubled her, and he didn't even know it. She proceeded to explain in great detail how she'd recreated Tuck and Colin's favorite treat. For once she felt someone other than a fellow scientist actually listened to her with true interest. Ian didn't nod blankly or hum here and there in agreement, he asked intelligent questions, added his own unique comments. Jenny hadn't enjoyed herself so much in a very long time. Well, except for their time in bed.

Ian slid his arm around her and pilfered a few more sweets.

"It looks like I'd better take these to Tuck before you eat them all," she said, and placed the treats into a container.

Ian took her arm as they made their way to Tuck's room.

"You are a wonder, sweeting. This is a truly magnificent achievement."

"If you're trying to butter me up so I'll make you a batch, it won't work," she said with a giggle.

He splayed one hand against his chest in mock surprise. "I am wounded that you would think so poorly of me."

She laughed and shook her head. "You're terrible. But you'll be happy to know that now that I have the recipe I'm going to show Maggie how they're made. You can place orders with her."

"I doubt she will be as accommodating as you," he said with a grin, and knocked on Tuck's door.

"Come in, anyone, someone!" Tuck called.

"I believe the lady is not in good spirits today," Ian said, and opened the door.

"Being confined to bed is not her idea of a good time."

"Ah, but your surprise will cheer her."

Tuck was indeed surprised. Ian had not seen her smile so bright in a long time. When Colin entered and she presented him with the treats, he nearly stuffed the lot of them into his mouth at once.

"I thank you, Jenny. 'Tis sad thing tae be so addicted tae such as these," he said, and pulled the bowl from Ian's reach. "Get your own, Sassenach."

Ian tsked. "An old dog with his bone has better manners than you."

Jenny laughed and pulled Ian out of the room. "You'll have your own soon enough. Now Tuck needs to rest."

"Tuck needs to have these babies!" Amelia called out as they closed the door.

"Aye, then maybe we can have a bit of peace!" Colin bellowed.

"They are so right for one another it's almost scary," Jenny said softly.

"Aye that they are." He swallowed hard, his moment of opportunity couldn't be better.

She stopped just inside her room. "Ian, are you all right?"

He realized he'd stopped in the doorway, his body not responding to anything his brain was telling it to do. All his energies were bolstering his courage. What if Amelia had been wrong? What if Jenny did wish for a title? What if his illegitimacy concerned her? What if...

What if she didn't love him?

"What is it? What's wrong?" She stepped closer, a pensive frown on her face.

"Will you be my wife?" Ian blurted out.

"What?"

"Will you be my wife?" he asked again, his voice nearly a whisper. She did not seem overly ecstatic with the question as he noted tears filling her eyes.

"How did you find out about the baby? How did you— never mind, you know. That much is obvious. It's logical considering everything," she said her voice quavering. "Well, it's of no consequence. I can handle the baby by myself."

All feeling went out of his limbs and he gripped the doorframe. "What?" he croaked.

"But thank you for asking," she said, ducking her head to the side. "It was noble of you."

His heart jolted and set his blood to boiling. He would not be his father! "Noble? No consequence? Like bloody hell 'tis of no consequence!"

"It's none of your concern."

"None of my—we will be wed at the earliest opportunity," he bit out.

"We will not!"

"I will not have my child born out of wedlock! I will not—" he swallowed down the bile creeping up his gullet. "I will not let my son be born a bastard," he hissed.

"Single mothers aren't uncommon in my time, and that's where he or she will be born. Legitimacy isn't an issue."

"You will not be taking my child away from me! Do you understand me, woman?"

"Oh! I'll go where I like, *when* I like, and you have nothing to say about it!"

"I have plenty to say about it!"

A sharp whistle split the air, and they both turned to Colin standing in the hallway, his hands braced on his hips. "I doona have a care what you two are fightin' over now, but do it somewhere else!"

"Sorry," Jenny said, then turned back to Ian. "The answer is still no." She slammed the door in Ian's face. He raised his fist to pound on it, but Colin eyed him, and not warmly.

"Bloody female," he groused as he stormed off, furious and profoundly hurt. Did she not care for him at all? And what of their child? How could she not wish to protect their babe from the cruelties of the world?

He made his way to the stables in search of something to ease the troubles in his mind, although he feared nothing, not even mucking out stalls would distract him.

****

Days later and they'd not spoken a word to one another. The nights were cold and lonely without Jenny by his side. Seeing her everyday and knowing she cared not for him was pure torment. And as the days marched on and she grew round with his child, he would be forced to watch from a distance, never touching her, holding her, feeling the movement of his child in her womb. How was he to bear the pain? And how would he survive when she left his world with his babe, his family?

"I think I may no' be well," Michael said, his voice shaky.

"Buck up, lad," Colin said, slapping him on the back as they all walked to the front of the little church where the priest stood. "'Tis naught but the rest of your life," he jested.

The rest of his life, Ian thought. If he were to but have that chance with Jenny. He forced a smile to his face. "You have naught to fear, lad. Look you how Colin has fared. All will be well."

Michael nodded with a sickening smile on his somewhat green face as he took his place in front of the priest with Colin at his side.

Ian sat beside Amelia in the first pew with Jenny on her other side. She had allowed Amelia this outing, but then no one would have been able to stop her from seeing Michael and Fiona's wedding. Nor did they wish to try.

Ian helped Amelia stand as the bagpipes began to play signaling the bride's entrance. Ian looked down the aisle as Fiona appeared in the doorway looking more beautiful than ever.

He cast a glance in Jenny's direction, his heart aching anew at the knowledge she would never walk down the aisle to him. Her gaze met his for but a moment, then turned swiftly back to Fiona as she joined Michael at the altar.

Once they were seated the priest began. His solemn tone rang through Ian's bones and he cast his eyes back to Jenny. She held his heart, his soul...his future. How could he bare to go through his life without her and their child a part of it?

She glanced his way and his heart lurched. Were those tears in her eyes? Was the touching scene before them calling to her heart as it called to his? He prayed it was so, for if it was so then she may have some feelings for him after all. His mind tumbled over the many ways in which he could persuade her to marry him. Sadly, none of them included a bed, but he would do his best to win her over.

A stray tear slid down her cheek, and she turned her head. He watched as she wiped it away with a quivering hand. Aye, he would pursue her affections. He had to. She was his world and he would be lost without her in it.

****

Jenny sniffled, hating how easily the ceremony stirred her. Although seeing Ian in his fine clothes hadn't helped. She missed him terribly. If only he hadn't ruined things with his guilty proposal.

She sighed silently. That was a lie. Even if he hadn't proposed, things would've changed between them. To be honest, she was surprised he was still here. She'd thought with her refusal, he'd hop on his horse and move on to someone else and not return until she was gone. Her and the baby.

Her eyes found his again. She wasn't sure what to think about the way he watched her, the soft smile on his face. She'd thought she'd seen pain there, but knew it was just her imagination. He may be agitated about her refusal, and he wasn't very happy to learn he was about to become a father, but she didn't think for a minute that he wanted to marry her for real. He felt honor bound to propose, it was as simple as that.

She let her mind wander for a moment, trying to imagine what it would be like to be Ian's wife. At first it would be pleasant. They could wake together every morning after having made love all night, instead of him slipping out of her room before sunrise. They would take long walks, have long talks, argue over theories. But as the days wore on and she got bigger, he would likely find another woman to spend his time with. Her body, large with child, would no longer entice him in the least.

Applause broke her from her thoughts. Michael led Fiona down the aisle a broad smile on his face. The sound of the pipes, intending to be joyful, sounded lonely to her ears. But she forced a watery smile to her face, not wanting to do anything to spoil their day.

Colin helped Amelia to her feet and walked her out of the church. Jenny started to follow when Ian quickly took her hand and slipped it into the crook of his arm. She shot him a glare and tried to pull free.

"Easy, love," he said softly. "Let us not make a scene in church."

She let him guide her outside and into the main hall where a feast was laid out for the couple. Ian didn't let go of her until she was seated at her place at the table. Unfortunately, he sat beside her.

Why would he suddenly be nice to her after she'd flatly refused his proposal? She knew she'd hurt his ego. His grumbling around the castle for the last few days was proof of that. But why the sudden change? It was a new puzzle. One she intended to solve.

"I don't know what you're up to, but it won't work," she whispered.

"I am up to naught but to make certain you do not overtax yourself." He leaned close to her ear. "You carry my child in your womb, little one. It would be remiss of me to not care for you."

Care for you. If only he did, if only he loved her as she loved him. If only it wasn't his honor, his pride at stake.

"I'm fine," she snapped. "I don't need you or anyone else looking after me. I'm a doctor, remember?"

He took her hand and pressed a kiss to the back. "And as I recall, doctors make the worst patients," he said with a wink, then placed a filled trencher in front of her.

"I can't eat all that."

"You shall try, sweeting. 'Tis what is best for you, both of you," he added with a whisper.

"I know how to take care of myself."

He sighed and looked at her, his eyes filled with—could it be pain?

"You will not allow me my child when the time comes. Is it so much to ask that I have some part in his life now?"

Her throat tightened. He may not love her, but he did care about her. They'd become close friends, and perhaps it wasn't impossible for him to care for his unborn child.

She nodded and lifted a small morsel to her lips, not tasting anything.

"Och, glad I am tae see you've made up," Elspeth said, patting them both on the back. "I've no' cared for the scowls you've both been wearin' these past days." She moved on to take her seat next to the Laird.

"Aye," Ian said with a broad smile. "I have not cared for the like either." He brushed the backs of his fingers across Jenny's cheek. "Might I have but one smile, sweeting? 'Tis a happy occasion."

She gave him a small one.

"Nay, I would much prefer one that reached your beautiful eyes."

She shook her head with a giggle. He was charming her, the rogue. And she loved every second of it.

Chapter Fourteen

The festivities went on for ages, then came to an abrupt halt as Tuck got to her feet and said, "Fiona, Michael, congrats on tying the not, but I've got to duck out of this party. I've got an appointment I can't break."

Colin jumped to his feet. "Now?" he asked and wrapped his arm around his wife. Tuck nodded with a grim smile.

Jenny rushed to her friend's side. "How far apart?"

"Ten minutes."

"You've been in labor for hours, haven't you?"

Tuck laughed roughly as Colin gave her support on one side while Jenny was on the other guiding her to the stairs. "You betcha. I didn't want to ruin the wedding. Can we move this train along? I don't know how much longer these guys are going to wait."

Colin gave Jenny a nod and scooped Tuck up and strode up the stairs to their chamber. Jenny, Elspeth, and Ian followed with blessings and prayers from the crowd.

Once Amelia was settled, Jenny started barking out orders. Ian was amazed. She was a sight to see, and he was ridiculously proud of her.

It was only a matter of moments before he and Colin were ordered from the room. Although Amelia had told him that men in her time stayed and assisted during the birthing, when Colin turned green after the first major pain, she decided it might be better if he didn't. But Colin did not seem to be taking the order well.

"Ian, get him out of here. And keep him out," Jenny instructed. "No matter what, understand?"

"Aye, love. I will not fail you." He kissed her quickly then pulled his large friend, and with no little effort, from the room.

Amelia's moans followed them through the door.

Colin fought against Ian's hold, but he would not relent. Jenny had given him a task, one he knew was important.

"Let me go, Sassenach!"

"Nay! You cannot go in there, you bloody Scot! You shall only be in the way!"

Another moan bled through the door. Ian had to get Colin out of hearing range or else he'd have to knock the man unconscious.

"Come, let us have something to drink while we wait." With Herculean effort, he pulled Colin down the corridor to the solar where he might manage his charge more effectively.

"I'll no' leave her!"

"You shall be no more than a few strides away. Jenny has told me these things can take hours. She knows her skill. Have faith, man!"

His large shoulders slumped, his head dropped to his chest. "Aye, faith." He followed Ian into the solar and made for the bottle of whiskey. He poured two generous drafts and handed Ian a cup. Colin tossed his back then sank to a chair, the look of a man beaten.

"All will be well," Ian said.

"I pray you are right, my friend. I pray you are right."

****

Hours later Jenny wiped her brow and fell into a chair by the hearth in Tuck's room. She'd sent Elspeth after Colin, having little strength to go get him herself. Mother and children were doing fine. Although early by at least a month, the babies would be fine. She'd watch them closely for the next month or so, but they were a good size and had healthy lungs as their wailing attested to.

Colin burst into the room, immense joy on his haggard face. He fell to his knees by Tuck at the head of the bed, a baby in each of her arms.

"I'd like you to meet your son and daughter," Tuck said, her eyes misty.

"Such wee things." One of the babies let out a cry, and Colin laughed. "With braw lungs."

Jenny's gaze shifted to Ian standing at the foot of the bed watching their friends. God, help her. She'd never seen such a look of longing in her life. How could she take his child away? And what would she tell their child when he asked about his father?

"Ian, come have a look at your godchildren," Tuck said.

Ian moved on unsteady legs to the opposite side of the bed. "They are beautiful, Amelia." He glanced at Colin. "'Tis a lucky happenstance that they did not take after their father."

Colin shot him a half-hearted glare, but there was little that could touch the immense joy emanating from him. Not even a teasing comment.

"You'd best watch yourself, Sassenach. My son will put you tae shame in the lists when he's of age."

"You'd better not be thinking that our daughter won't be allowed in the lists, MacLean," Amelia said.

Colin chuckled. "Nay, mavourneen. She will have the entire keep wrapped around her finger. I've no doubt of it."

Ian turned his attention back to the babes. He'd held his half-sister's child once, the only member of his family who cared for him, and had been more than proud to be an uncle. Her husband had not been quite as congenial as his sister, placing a pall on the entire affair, but this was something different. His dearest friends were now parents and had chosen him to be the children's godfather. He could not be more proud. Nor could he deny the painful longing burning in his chest.

His gaze turned to Jenny sitting quietly by the fire. His child, his babe was nestled in his love's womb not but a few feet from where he sat. And he could not make them his.

He'd never know the joy he'd seen on Colin's face. He would never know the joy of a woman's love, one whom he loved with all his heart and soul.

His eyes misted over with pain. She had said no, and he did not wish to renew the pain with another rejection. But she did carry his child and her fatigue was evident. She had at least given him some leave to take part in the child's well being while she remained in his time.

Ian cleared his throat and kissed Amelia on the forehead. "Congratulations, dear heart."

He moved across the room to where Jenny sat. "You should be abed," he said, taking her hand and pulling her to her feet.

"I'm fine."

"You have dark circles under your eyes. 'Tis obvious that the birthing has taxed you greatly. You should be resting."

"In a little while."

She started to move away, but he snagged her by the arm. "Nay. Now."

Her face flushed with annoyance. "I'm the doctor around here, and I say when I need to rest."

"And I am the father of our child, and I say you need to rest now."

Jenny gasped, while Colin, the unhelpful sod, chortled. Amelia, however, was not happy. "Ian Southernland, I am going to kill you," she growled. "You promised—"

"I have asked for her hand, but she refuses me!" That took the anger from Amelia's face and replaced it with one of pure mystification.

"Jen?" Amelia asked.

"I won't marry him just because I'm pregnant," she bit out tearfully, and looked at him. "You don't want to marry me. Not really."

"I do."

"No, you don't. You have scores of women to choose from, there's no logical reason to choose me."

Cupping her cheek, he leaned closer. "Love isn't logical."

"You don't love me. You just feel guilty," she said, tears flowing down her cheeks as she ran from the room.

He should not have tried, but every time he saw her, caught a whiff of her scent on the air, he was lost.

"She's just confused, Ian," Amelia said. "She'll come around, I'm sure of it."

He shook his head and cast her and Colin a grim smile. "Would that were true," he said, and left the room.

He stood atop the castle for ages, ignoring the wind whipping at his clothes, chilling his body, but 'twas nothing compared to the chill in his soul. She would never have him. She could not be convinced he would be true to her and only her. If he could only undo the past, but even then he feared the true cause of her rejection was not his past roguish ways. She did not love him, not in truth. Not as he loved her.

Chapter Fifteen

Jenny stared out the large window in the solar to the rolling hills, wondering if her heart would ever feel the same again.

"There you be," Colin said. "Amelia wishes tae have a word with you."

"Tell her I'll check in later, Colin. I'm really not up to it right now."

He snagged her hand and dragged her from the room. "If you doona come with me now, my wife will be comin' tae fetch you herself."

"But—"

"Now, in you go," he said, shoving her into the room.

"Why you ever married that man will forever be a mystery," she grumbled.

Tuck laughed. "We're a lot a like."

"No kidding," she said, and flopped down into a chair. "Okay, present your arguments, your commiserations, your theories, and so forth so I can go to bed," she lied. Bed was the last place she wanted to be. It reminded her of Ian and she found she couldn't sleep a wink in the blasted thing. Or maybe she just wouldn't ever sleep again. Not after today and that look on his face.

"He loves you," Tuck said plainly.

Jenny shook her head. "No. He doesn't."

Tuck sighed. "Okay, so you want proof. He asked you to marry him."

"Because I'm pregnant."

"I don't believe that."

"Well, it isn't your place to believe or disbelieve," she snapped. She leaned forward and rubbed her face. "I'm sorry, Tuck. I'm just tired."

"And in love."

She shook her head, but couldn't voice a denial.

"Jenny, not long after you got back, I asked him what

was up between you too. After I set him straight on a few things, he admitted that his heart was involved. He was afraid you wouldn't *welcome his suit*, which I can only assume means a proposal. That, according to my count, was long before you figured out you were pregnant."

"What do you mean he was afraid?"

Tuck sighed and grinned. "The big dummy thought you'd be bothered by his status. He's got no lands, no title, and he's illegitimate." Her grin faded. "I told him you didn't care about any of that. Was I wrong?"

Her head ached. "No, you weren't wrong." She massaged her temples. "But that still doesn't mean—"

"Jenny, the man is in love with you. And you're in love with him. Don't blow this with some twisted logic. He swore to me he'd be faithful, and I for one, believe him."

"What if you're wrong?"

"Then you end up with a broken heart. But how is that any worse than the one you've got now?"

Jenny lifted her head, a small grin on her face. "You know that's almost logical."

"I do have my moments," Tuck said with a snort.

"I'll think about it. Now get some rest. Doctor's orders."

"You too."

Jenny wandered the corridors until she found herself atop the castle over looking the loch, the setting sun sent yellow spears of light across the waters. The wind bit at her skin, but she paid no attention to it. Her brain was generating enough heat to throw off the seasons.

Did he really love her? Would he be faithful? Was she just letting her fears stop her from being happy? True he had played the field rather heavily, but not once since they'd met had he seemed interested in other women. There was that night in Edinburgh when he got drunk, however, but she had no proof he'd been with a woman. He's said he was with the peddler and the man did in fact show the next day.

But was he sincere? The same question she asked herself a million times when dealing with the opposite sex. She couldn't tell when they lied or not. It was beyond frustrating. But Tuck believed him. Colin trusted him. Elspeth adored him. Did he really want her?

Possibly. The odds were...

"To hell with the odds," she grumbled. Sooner or later someone always won the lottery. Maybe it was her turn...or not, but standing there wondering about it wasn't going to do her any good. The answers weren't floating in the loch.

With a newfound determination, she turned to the stairs, eager to find Ian, and came face to face with Vernon Cox.

"I'm glad to see you're in such a hurry," he said, the gun pointing straight at her.

She eased back several steps.

He snickered. "I know there's no way off this roof but behind me, so you might as well give up." Jenny didn't move. "It's time to go home and pay Daddy a visit."

Her brow furrowed. "Why? What is it you want, Vernon?"

"Only what's due me."

Jenny saw a shadow from the corner of her eye in the small alcove beside the stairway. "And what would that be," she said, stalling him, hoping to heaven it wasn't Fiona or Elspeth, but one of the guards.

"My name belongs on EQ13!" He pounded his chest, his face red with rage. "I discovered it! Not you and not your father!"

"Really, Vernon, it's just a diet pill."

An unnatural laugh gurgled from his throat. "You're wrong."

She needed to change her strategy, insulting the man wasn't very smart. But then lately she didn't feel very smart about much of anything. "Um, I was under the impression you sold it to my father."

"He stole it! He tricked me into signing everything over to him!"

"I see, and you think that by kidnapping me, you can force him to tear up the contracts? Not likely, Vernon."

"He'll do more than that. Now that I've got a gateway to the past, I'll fix it so his entire empire belongs to me."

"Then you don't need me."

He grinned crookedly. "I need you to make the gateway work."

"Well that might be a problem. You see it only works

on the Solstice and it only comes here," she lied, having no idea if it went to other time periods. But she felt certain, even with Ian's rather interesting theories on the operation of the loops that it still only worked on the solstice.

"You're lying," he hissed.

"I am afraid the lady is correct," Ian said, stepping out of the alcove directly between her and Vernon. "She cannot make the portal work. And the next solstice is—"

"Five months, six days, sixteen hours, and twenty-nine minutes."

Ian cast her a grin. "Thank you, love. 'Twould seem you have now begun to finish my sentences."

She shrugged with a small smile.

"No, you're both lying. You're just trying to trick me, like I did those stupid McKenzies."

Ian sighed. "Little man, you are sorely trying my patience. I do—not—lie," he growled.

Jenny's heart flipped and tripped all over itself. No, Ian didn't lie. The outrageous flattery he showered on Elspeth and others was the closest thing to a lie to ever leave his lips, and even then there was always a bit of truth to them.

"No, you don't, do you?" she whispered, completely stunned that she hadn't seen the truth from the beginning.

Ian turned, blocking her from Vernon's view completely. "Nay, I do not. I have seen the immense pain a lie can inflict."

The image of him rushing toward her when Vernon had grabbed her at Tobor Morar, the look on his face when he'd laid her on the bed with a bullet hole in her leg, the many moments she'd had with him rushed before her mind's eye. He did not lie, which meant...

"Move, Southernland. I didn't tolerate the cold nights, the harsh work, a stinking cesspit of a dungeon, to let anything or anyone stand in my way."

She swallowed the burgeoning fear before it could take over her mind. "Ian. Step aside."

"Nay." His gaze bored into hers. "I will not let him harm you."

"I'll shoot you. I swear I will," Vernon said, his voice

shaky.

Jenny shook her head, almost frantically, the fear of losing Ian now nearly overtaking her. "Ian, please. He won't hurt me. He needs me." She took one wobbly step to the side, easing around him.

"Nay!" He spun around and threw himself at Vernon before she could take another step.

The gun went off and Jenny screamed. She rushed to Ian lying atop Vernon on the cold stone, neither of them moving. With quivering hands, she reached for Ian just as he rolled over. Blood covered his doublet and she fell to her knees beside him, her hands running over him frantically. Where was the cool calm doctor? Why couldn't she be who she needed to be?

"Nay, love. 'Tis not my blood." He caught her hands in his and pressed them to his chest. "I am unharmed."

Jenny's gaze slid to the side to Vernon's lifeless body then jumped back to Ian. The man had thrown himself into the line of fire for her. "You really do love me."

"Aye, love. With all my heart."

She shook her head as tears poured down her cheeks. "I'm so stupid."

He chuckled hoarsely. "Nay, just stubborn."

"Oh, Ian," she cried, and buried her face against his neck, her body trembling.

"Take care of him, lads," he said to the guards who'd come running at the sound of the shot. He climbed to his feet, lifting her into his arms, and hurried to her room.

Carefully, he placed her on the edge of the bed. She didn't know where the shaking came from, but she couldn't seem to stop.

"Here." He pressed a cup to her lips and she sipped it.

She looked into his worried eyes, so blue, so beautiful, and he was hers. It seemed so incredibly impossible, but it was true. "I'm all right. It's just a little shock. Vernon—me—you. All this time I didn't see—I didn't believe. Oh, Ian. I'm so sorry I doubted you."

He nodded and ran his finger down the side of her cheek. "'Tis in the past, love. And your doubt was not completely unfounded. I do have a bit of a reputation," he said with a rough chuckle. "But I have been thinking," he said softly.

She smiled. "Dangerous occupation."

"Cheeky woman. You will not deter me from this," he said with a grin. "I asked you to be my wife, but I fear I have not done so in a manner pleasing to your ears." His smile fell as he studied their linked hands in her lap. "'Tis true that I have no prospects, no title, and am a bastard by birth. But I have ne'er lied to you, nor will I e'er be unfaithful. I love you, Jenny Maxwell, with all my heart. All my soul. So I ask you, once again, to consent to be my bride. If you do not love me, then I will ask no more." He looked at her, his eyes filled with uncertainty. "Do you love me?"

"But I can't stay in this time," she choked out.

"Then we shall go forward, backward, I care not which, as long as we are together. Do—you—love—me?"

She nodded, tears flowing down her cheeks.

He leaned forward and whispered against her lips. "Then marry me. I beg you."

"Yes." She threw her arms around his neck and kissed him with everything she had in her.

Colin appeared in the doorway. "I take it the lass is well," Colin said.

Ian lifted his head and smiled at his friend. "Aye, all is as it should be. Tell Amelia that Jenny is fine and has consented to be my wife."

"And you'd better hurry before she gets out of bed to find out for herself," Jenny added tearfully.

Chuckling, Colin closed the door behind him.

Ian eased onto the bed beside her and pulled her into his lap, her head nestled beneath his chin. "We have much to discuss," he said, and cleared his throat, the topic not of his liking. "Amelia has told me much of your life. About your work, your father...your fortune. But I have naught to give you, Jen. Nothing but my sorry self and a few coins."

She lifted her head and peered into his eyes while stealing her arms around his neck. "And that bothers you."

"Aye, greatly. Your sire will look upon me and ask me of my worth and I have nothing to commend me."

"The fact that you saved my life, that I love you, that you're the father of my child...none of those things count.

Is that what you mean?"

He leaned his forehead against hers with a sigh. "The fact that I bedded you before wedding you is most definitely not in my favor. But 'tis my lack of prospects that concerns me most."

She kissed him tenderly. "Then we will have to do something about that, Master Southernland."

"And how do you propose we do that, Mistress Maxwell?" he whispered, returning her kiss and lingering at the sweet edges of her lips.

On a moan she tilted back her head and allowed him access to her neck as he trailed kisses across her skin. "We need to examine your talents and exploit them."

He chuckled as he nipped her shoulder with his teeth. "I do not think I can increase my coffers with this particular talent."

With a laugh she pushed at his shoulders. "I am not about to comment on that, but you do have other talents."

"Talents we shall discuss at a later time, love," he said, and laid her on the bed where they ended a day filled with life and death with some very pleasurable pursuits.

Chapter Sixteen

"Have you figured out anything yet?" Tuck asked.

Jenny handed little Heather back to her mother. "No. Every idea I or Colin has, Ian shoots down without a thought. I'm almost afraid we'll never get married."

"Hey, this isn't stopping him from saying I do, is it?"

Jenny nodded with a grim frown.

"Oh, you've definitely got to find something for him to do then."

"I know," she sighed. "He refuses to step into the future with nothing to show for himself. He has too much pride to go to my father with nothing. And he hates the idea of me paying for everything when we get there."

"He wants to work," Tuck said with a snort. "A day I never thought I'd see."

Jenny planted her hands on her hips and looked across to Tuck where she nursed Heather. "You make it sound like he's lazy."

She chuckled. "No, not lazy, just privileged."

"If only one of his apprenticeships could do him some good in the future," she said thoughtfully.

"I don't think sixteenth century law will do him any good."

"No, not unless he writes history books." Jenny threw up her hand before Tuck could suggest it. "I already mentioned it, and no. He doesn't see himself as a writer or expert on history. Too stodgy, he says."

Tuck nodded with a crooked grin. "Yeah, I have to admit. I can't see him as something that—settled. He likes activity, fighting, riding—"

Jenny laughed. "And charming whoever is around."

"Hey, how about politician?"

"Are you kidding? He'd probably challenge his opponent to a duel the first time a derogatory remark was made about him."

"Or you or your father." Tuck sighed and tucked Heather into the crib beside her brother. "No. I'm afraid that man has knowledge of only three things that will carry to the future. Ancient weaponry, women, and horses."

Jenny stilled. "Horses?"

She sat back in her chair and adjusted her gown. "Sure. He spent all his time in stables when he wasn't working in the lists or chasing skirts. I think he still does."

Her head cocked to the side as ideas raced through her mind. "And you're certain he wasn't just sneaking off to the stables with a girl?"

"Positive. To be honest, he hasn't done much chasing since I got back last fall. I don't think he likes to fool around with the locals. Too messy if things should go bad, know what I mean?"

A smile spread across Jenny's face as the perfect solution to the problem came to her. "Tuck, you're a genius." With that she jumped out of her chair and bolted through the door.

"Thanks! But what did I say?"

****

Ian pitched another bit of muck from the stall into a cart, his body drenched with sweat. He'd shed his doublet and shirt ages ago, but could not shed his apprehension. Hard work oft settled his brain when a problem presented itself, but not this time. After a few hours in the lists, then a long hard ride, he'd resorted to mucking stalls to find some relief, but to no avail.

"Ian, I—" Jenny stopped but a few paces inside the stable, her mouth agape.

"What is it?" He dropped the shovel and hurried to her. "Are you not well?" He pressed his dirt-smudged hand against her belly. "Is the babe all right?"

A slow sweet smile spread across her lips. "I love you. Do you know that?"

"Aye, but—"

She threw her arms around his neck and kissed him soundly.

"Sweet Jen," he moaned, relishing the feel of her in his arms, in his heart. "I fear I am getting your dress

169

dirty," he whispered against her lips.

"I don't care," she sighed.

With a chuckle, he pulled away, but only a scant bit of inches. "And the need for a kiss is what brought you running into the stables, scaring me half out of my wits?"

"Mmm, I always need your kisses. Especially when you look so incredibly sexy without your shirt." She kissed him, rubbing against him like a kitten, then pulled free of his arms. "But I do have another reason for being here."

"Aye, and have tortured me soundly for it."

She giggled with an impish gleam in her eye. "I'd say I'm sorry, but we both know that would be a lie."

"You shall pay the price later, my love." He kissed the tip of her nose then returned to the shovel. "So what is this reason for seeking me out other than torture?"

"I've solved the problem."

He slowly turned back to her, banking the hope growing in his chest. The need to be worthy of her was all he could think on. He could protect her, but could not provide for her and their babe, not in her time.

"Horses."

Ian blinked a moment or two. "Horses?"

She nodded, her eyes bright, her smile wide.

"I am afraid, love you shall have to explain. Horses are not a means of travel in your time. How could they be the answer to my problem?"

"Horses may not be for everyday travel, but they're widely used for pleasure. Some places still use them for work, like in America."

He shook his head, not understanding her logic. "I cannot care for you and our child mucking stalls."

"No, not that. You know all about them. Breeding, training, buying, trading, you know it all."

"Aye, I have a vast knowledge of the beasts, but horse breeding is not an inexpensive venture. I would need the funds to begin, which I do not have." He put away the shovel and took up his clothes as he crossed to her. "I am sorry, love. 'Tis a fine idea, truly, but I cannot undertake such an endeavor."

"How much?"

"Nay, you will not provide it, nor will I ask Colin for it," he said firmly. "We shall think of something else."

"No. This is the answer, I'm certain of it."

He put his arm around her waist and started across the bailey.

"Ian, how much money do you think you have to have in your pocket to feel comfortable marrying me?"

He stopped in mid-stride. "You think that—nay, love. You have it wrong." Pulling her into his arms, ignoring the jeers from the battlements, he kissed her. How could she think that he would not honor his vow? "Nothing will stop me from marrying you. Not my station, not my empty purse, nothing this side of death will stop me from having you as my wife."

"Do you mean it?"

"Aye, my love. With all my heart. I only wish to provide for you without aid, 'tis a matter of pride. I will wed you, make no mistake."

His fingers drifted down her long braid as his gaze roamed o'er her fey features. If he had but known this was why she'd not chosen their wedding date, he would have explained himself ages ago. "You have but to say when. And I warn you, little one. If you do not pick the date before sundown this day, I will toss you o'er my shoulder and present you before the priest first thing on the morrow."

With a smile so bright and tears in her eyes, she said, "How fast can you get cleaned up?"

Ian threw back his hair with a boisterous laugh. "Today it shall be."

****

Nestled together in the marriage bed, Ian let his fingers drift over her shoulder, along her arm, down to the hand that wore his ring. He lifted it and placed a kiss to the back of his wife's hand.

Wife. The word had meant little to him in the past, but today, this night, and for the rest of his life it would mean heaven.

"You're thinking again," he whispered, spying the small crease between her brows.

"You never gave me a price." She turned on her side and cupped his face, running her thumb across his bottom lip. "How much do you need to feel comfortable?"

"You have no need to worry on that, love. I will have

enough before we leave."

"Oh?"

"Colin has need of new horse flesh and does not wish to leave Amelia and the babes. I will go in his stead."

"You're going to act as his buyer?"

"Aye."

She smiled as she kissed him. "Then when we get home, you can begin building your own lines, and you will be using my dowry to help you." He shook his head, but she stayed him. "Yes, you will. That's how it's done now, and that's how it will be done when we get home."

With a chuckle, he kissed her. "And how much, dare I ask, is your dowry?"

"Whatever is fair for this century."

"Why do I detect an omission?"

"Oh, all right, this century plus a cost of living increase."

He laughed and settled atop her lithe form. "Four hundred years is quite a lot of increase, think you?"

"It's only fair," she said breathlessly, as he sheathed himself in her warmth.

"Aye, fair in deed. I shall not let you win every argument, love."

"Mmm, who's arguing?"

Note from the author...

Tobor Morar is a real port. It was not actually established, however, until the late 1700s.

Still Waters

by

Jo Barrett

The roughness of a new beard scraped against Joanna's skin as thick full lips pressed firmly against her mouth. She whimpered and the pressure softened. Slowly he pulled away, but she didn't want him to leave. It had been three years since a man had really kissed her, and although it hadn't felt like the start of a kiss, she desperately wished it to end as one. After all, she was only dreaming again.

She often had dreams like this one. Dreams where a faceless man held her in his arms and soothed her aching spirit. She used to see her husband's face, and in the beginning, that had brought her comfort, but over the years since his death, his image had faded. Now there was no face, no identity, only the feeling, and she welcomed it.

With a soft moan, she caressed his lips. He lingered, barely touching, then pressed his mouth once more against hers. Teasing her lips apart, his tongue enticed hers to explore the taste and texture of his mouth, dueling and delving deeper, filling the emptiness of her weary soul. She wanted the feeling to last forever, but after another moment of pure bliss he was gone, and it was time to wake up.

Slowly lifting her heavy lids, she found herself looking into a pair of eyes the color of cool green moss.

"Welcome back." The deep resonant tone of his voice sent goose bumps across her damp skin and she shivered.

He raised his head and turned, giving her a view of his nearly perfect profile. "Toss me that towel."

Not a dream? Not a faceless lover?

A two-day-old beard covered his strong jaw and upper lip. Around his face and across his tanned brow, hair dark as pitch lay in unruly waves. Water droplets fell from the tips as he turned back to her. Stroking her skin with the towel, she shivered again.

"I hope you're not going into shock," he said.

Shock? She'd just experienced the most delicious kiss

of her life from the most handsome man she had ever seen.

Hell yes, she was in shock. But that wasn't what he meant. Her thoughts hurried back to the moment before she opened her eyes, but her mind was totally blank except for the kiss.

She cleared her throat awkwardly. "What happened?"

He leaned over her, stopping a whisper away. His lashes were long and spiked together with moisture. She felt lost in his eyes.

"You almost drowned. You bumped your head and went under. I pulled you out. I was about to give you mouth-to-mouth resuscitation." His thick full lips cocked into a rakish grin. "Or I thought I was. I guess you didn't take in any water after all."

Was it possible to die from embarrassment? Joanna briefly touched her mouth with her fingers. A faint taste of lake water lingered across her tongue, but her throat and lungs felt fine.

"How do you feel?" he asked.

A bead of water fell from a lock of hair curling out from his brow, landing on her cheek. He gently brushed away the moisture with the tip of his finger as though he were sweeping away a dewdrop from a flower.

"A-All right, I guess," she said.

"Glad to hear it." He smiled widely, uncovering a set of straight white teeth, a bright contrast to his shadowed chin and tan skin.

She could feel his warm breath fanning her damp cheeks and absently licked her lips, remembering the feel of his mouth pressed against hers only moments ago. Her eyes lingered over his mouth as she let the memory warm her in all sorts of forgotten places. The stranger's broad smile faded, pulling her gaze back to his. Something hovered between them as they studied one another. Something she hadn't felt in a very long time.

Sexual attraction.

About the author...

Jo currently resides in North Carolina with her patient and supportive family while she juggles her writing career and her position as a programmer analyst. In her early years, she wrote folk songs, poetry, and an occasional short story or two, but never dreamed of writing a book. She didn't even like to read! But one fateful day, she picked up a romance novel and found herself hooked. Not only did she discover the joy of reading, but the joy of writing books. These days, if she isn't tapping away at her computer on a story of her own, she has her nose buried in the latest romance novel hot off the presses, and is enjoying every minute of it.

She participates regularly in a critique group, and attends various seminars and classes, constantly honing her writing skills, determined to squeeze as much time into developing her craft as she does creating new stories about the quest for love. Someday, she hopes to take off her programming hat and write full time. So many of her dreams have already come true. What's one more?

Visit Jo's website at www.jobarrett.net

LaVergne, TN USA
26 January 2010
171119LV00004B/8/P